Big & Little Questions
(ACCORDING TO WREN JO BYRD)

Big & Little Questions

(According to Wren Jo Byrd)

BY
JULIE BOWE

kd

Kathy Dawson Books

KATHY DAWSON BOOKS

PENGUIN YOUNG READERS GROUP

An imprint of Penguin Random House LLC

375 Hudson Street

New York, NY 10014

Library of Congress Cataloging-in-Publication Data

Names: Bowe, Julie, date, author.

Title: Big & little questions (according to Wren Jo Byrd) / Julie Bowe.

Description: New York, NY : Kathy Dawson Books, 2017. | Summary: "Fourth grader
Wren Jo Byrd questions lots of things—both little and big—when her parents decide
to get a divorce, and learns a lot about the true meaning of family, home, and
friendship"— Provided by publisher.

Identifiers: LCCN 2016013897 | ISBN 9780803736931 (hardcover)

Subjects: | CYAC: Questions and answers—Fiction. | Family problems—Fiction.
| Divorce—Fiction. | Friendship—Fiction.

Classification: LCC PZ7.B671943 Bep 2017 | DDC [Fic]—dc23

LC record available at https://lccn.loc.gov/2016013897

Printed in the United States of America

1 3 5 7 9 10 8 6 4 2

Design by Jennifer Kelly

Text set in Apollo MT Std

Who is the best editor in the world?
♥ Kathy Dawson. ★
This book is for her.

★ Contents ★

Big & Little Questions
(ACCORDING TO WREN JO BYRD)

CHAPTER 1

★

Can Two Make a Family?

Lots of things have changed since my last first week of school.

- Most of my baby teeth have fallen out and the big ones are filling in.
- My jeans still fit, but they are shorter.
- My hair is long enough to tie under my chin.
- I have a new favorite color—orange (sorry, blue).
- Amber and I got our ears pierced. (Afterward, we hyperventilated for a while.)
- My parents gave me my own phone. Amber has the same one.

But all those changes seem little compared to the big change that happened over the summer. Dad moved out. When your parents decide to get a divorce, someone has to leave.

Now big things—like meeting my new teacher, and finding my desk, and wondering if my friends are allowed to wear tinted lip gloss to school this year—seem little. And *little* things—like family photos disappearing from the refrigerator door, and not hearing Dad's truck pull into the driveway, and not smelling his spicy chili simmering on the stove—seem big.

First, Dad lived at a hotel. Then he moved in with some friends. Now it's September and he's renting a cabin across the lake from our house. I mean, *Mom's* house. I mean, my house. I mean, I don't know what I mean.

Mom and Dad told me they were getting a divorce on the first day of summer vacation, which used to be my favorite day of the year. I was eating a bowl of fruity cereal. I remember because as soon as they said that word—*divorce*—I dribbled pink milk down the front of my sparkly koala bear shirt. The one I got when Amber invited me to spend spring break at a resort with her family. We both got the same shirt and pretended we were sisters. Mom and Dad kept talking, but I stopped listening and ran to the bathroom and threw up even though I didn't have the flu or anything. Fruity cereal does not taste good on its way out of your stomach, but it's still just as bright.

Mom and Dad told me that everything would be okay, and nothing was my fault, and they both loved me very much.

But nothing was okay.

I'm part of this family too. I should get a say in the big stuff.

My mom is the head librarian at the Oak Hill Public Library, and she's always telling me to look things up for myself. I looked up the word *divorce* in the big, fat dictionary that sits on a fancy pedestal at the back of her library. It's not like I'd never heard that word before. I mean, I watch TV. But I didn't really know what it meant, or exactly how to spell it. After a few tries, I found it.

~~Davorse~~
~~Devorce~~
Divorce
- A complete separation between two things
- To dissolve a marriage

Then I looked up the word *dissolve.*

Dissolve
- To break up
- To melt
- To disappear

If you ask me, *dissolve* is a dumb word for divorce because it doesn't make things melt and disappear like ice cream or cotton candy. *Divorce* makes everything hard and sour, like a jawbreaker you have to keep hidden in your cheek so it doesn't get stuck in your throat.

After Dad started looking for a place to rent, and taught me how to use my new phone, Mom hauled a big suitcase down from the attic and told me I had to go stay with my grandparents in the city while she and Dad had lawyer meetings and divided up all their stuff.

I love G-ma and G-pa, but going away when everything was falling apart felt like the biggest mistake in the world. But I still had to go.

I missed Amber's birthday.

And swimming lessons.

And fireworks over Pickerel Lake.

And Phoebe Bartlett's Fourth of July cookout.

And the summer reading party at the library.

Mom gave me hardly any warning, so there wasn't even time to say good-bye to anyone. I saw my school friends Phoebe and Eleanor riding their bikes when Mom was driving me to my grandparents' house. They were wearing swimsuits and flip-flops, with beach towels around their necks, so I knew they were on their way to the pool. Amber was probably meeting them there because we are all friends. I almost waved to them, but then I thought, *What if Mom stops so I can talk to them? How can I tell my friends I'm going away because my mom and dad are getting divorced?*

So I scrunched down in my seat as Mom drove past.

Amber sent me texts, but I didn't know how to answer. So I didn't.

When I finally got to come home, Dad's desk was gone. So was his recliner. There were gaps on our bookshelf, like missing teeth. His lucky baseball cap wasn't hanging on the hook by the back door, and none of his clothes were in the laundry. My favorite goofy picture of us—the one Mom took of him and me at the water park when I was finally big enough to go on the logjam ride—was nowhere. I guess it was Dad's favorite picture too.

Last night, Mom wrote a reminder and stuck it to the fridge with a smiley face magnet.

WREN'S WEEKLY SCHEDULE

MONDAY—THURSDAY: MEET MOM AT THE LIBRARY AFTER SCHOOL.

FRIDAY: RIDE BUS #5 TO YOUR DAD'S PLACE.

SATURDAY—SUNDAY: STAY WITH YOUR DAD.

I walk over to the fridge and turn the smiley face magnet upside down.

Mom already bought me another toothbrush, extra hair bands, and new pajamas. She packed them in the cinch sack I use for sleepovers. Before this summer, Amber and I had sleepovers practically every weekend. Her family is big and loud, but it never feels crowded there. Not like my house, which sometimes feels crowded even though only three people live here. I mean, two people now. Is two even enough for a family?

"Chop-chop, Wren," Mom says, taking a slice of pizza from the take-out box on the kitchen counter. "Family Night starts in fifteen minutes. I've got to make a couple phone calls, then we'll head over to school." She checks her phone for messages.

"What about Dad?" I ask. "Isn't he coming with us?"

"I already told you, Wren," Mom says, glancing up as she scrolls. "I gave him your schedule. He can meet us there."

"But why can't he come here first? There's lots of pizza. He's probably hungry."

"He's not hungry," Mom says.

"How do you know?" I ask. "Have you talked to him?"

Mom sighs and clicks off her screen. "No, Wren. But I'm sure he's eating supper at his . . . cabin. Now finish eating. We're running late."

Mom heads into the living room with her phone to her ear.

I push the pizza box away.

"Mew? *Meew?*" Shakespeare pitter-patters across the kitchen floor and rubs a figure eight around my ankles. I pick him up and stroke his pussy-willow-white fur. "No, I'm not hungry," I reply to my cat. "Yes, my stomach feels icky again."

When I hear Mom's voice a moment later, I let myself hope that it's Dad she's talking to. "Maybe she decided to call him," I whisper to Shakespeare. "There's still time for him to stop by. We can go together."

But then I hear Mom say big words like *interrogatories* and *financial portfolios* and *equalization of investments,* so I know it's just her lawyer again. They never use little words when they talk.

* * *

Shakespeare purrs and licks my cheek. His tongue feels as scratchy as Dad's whiskers used to feel at the end of the day.

Shakespeare meows again, and I give him a piece of pepperoni. It's against our family rules to feed him from the table. But I'm not eating at the table. I'm at the kitchen counter. And there's no real family here anymore anyway. It's just me.

CHAPTER 2

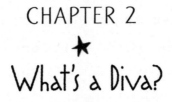

What's a Diva?

As we head out the door for Family Night, I ask Mom if I can bring Shakespeare along.

"No, Wren," she says. "Family Night is no place for a cat."

"But he can stay in the car until we're done. I'll put him in his carrier with some toys. Please? Can I?"

"Wren, I gave you my answer." Mom takes a little mirror and a lipstick from her purse and puts some on. She checks her reflection, then sighs like she isn't crazy about what she sees.

"But why can't Shakespeare come?" I persist. "If Dad were here, he wouldn't care."

"Your dad isn't here," Mom replies, snapping the clasp on her purse. "Now, chop-chop or we'll be late." She picks up her keys and opens the back door. "Grab a jacket, it's getting chilly."

Mom heads out.

I stomp behind her, leaving Shakespeare and my jacket at home.

On the way to my school, I call Amber. I've been texting her since I got back, but she hasn't answered me. I never called Amber from G-ma and G-pa's. Not once. Amber hates crying. I did a lot of crying over the summer.

I was hoping we could meet our new teacher together. We wanted Mr. Ortega because he's super-nice and wears funny ties and has an old-time popcorn machine in his classroom for Friday afternoon movies. But Amber, Phoebe, Eleanor, and I got Ms. Little instead. Mom showed me the class list that came in the mail when I was gone. Ms. Little is brand-new, so I don't know if she's nice or funny or if she even likes popcorn. At least I get to be with my friends.

Finally, on the fifth ring, Amber answers her phone.

"Hi, it's me," I say. "Didn't you get my messages?"

There's a pause, then Amber says, "Oh . . . hi. Yes, I got them. I was too busy to answer. You know how it is."

"Amber, I'm so sorry I didn't tell you I was going away. I was super-sad to miss your birthday."

"Not sad enough to call me or send a card," she says coolly.

"I started to text you a bunch of times . . . everything has been crazy lately . . . I—" But I can't talk about my messed-up family when Mom is in the car. "I . . . uh . . . how was everything while I was gone?"

"It. Was. *Excellent,*" Amber replies. "Except I am *So. Bummed.* I don't want school to start! Marianna and I went swimming *Ev-Ree Day.*"

I frown into my phone. "Why are you talking like a robot? Who is Marianna?"

"This is how I *talk* now, Wren," Amber says, like she bought a new voice when she did her school shopping. "Marianna moved to Oak Hill this summer. She is the coolest girl *Ev-Er.* A total *Dee-Va.*"

I'm not exactly sure what a diva is, but I think it has something to do with opera. Maybe the new girl likes to sing?

Amber starts gushing more details about Marianna. ". . . moved here from *Seattle . . . gobs* of friends . . . *tons* of cool clothes . . ."

I half listen as I take the phone away from my ear and lean forward so I can see Mom from the backseat. She's clenching the steering wheel even though there is almost no traffic. I notice she isn't wearing her wedding ring anymore. "Mom? What's a diva?"

Mom turns down the radio a notch and glances over her shoulder. "Look it up," she replies.

I sit back with a sigh.

Amber is still talking. *". . . and then Marianna double-dog dared me to hide some older boys' beach towels in the bushes! Oh-Em-Gee! We were laughing hysterically when they couldn't find them and had to drip all the way home . . ."*

I tap *D-E-E-V-A* into my phone's dictionary. It fixes my spelling mistake.

Diva
- A glamorous and popular female performer
- Prima donna
- Goddess
- Queen

Diva *means queen,* I say to myself. *I wonder if the new girl lives in a castle.*

"O-Em-*Gee*!" Amber's voice cuts through the hum the car. "Marianna just texted me! Later!"

I press the phone to my ear again. "Wait! I'm almost at the school. Meet me by the—"

But Amber is gone.

As Mom pulls into the Oak Hill Elementary parking lot a minute later, I see Amber thumbing her phone while walking inside with her parents, and Ivory and Slate, her sister and brother. Ivory goes to the middle school next door. Slate is starting kindergarten.

Lots of other kids are arriving with their families too. Oak Hill is small, so I recognize most of them as I look across the lot. I see Bo and Ty from my class, walking inside. Sometimes I call them Bowtie because they are always together. Bo's dad holds the door open for his mom and Ty's parents. And there's Ruby Olson, tossing a foam football around with her brothers; and Noah, another boy from my class. The Olsons' football bonks Noah's big sister on the head, so she hollers at them, and they all crack up.

The whole sidewalk is filling up with moms and dads walking together, and kids darting ahead, excited to show their families the way to their classrooms.

We get out of the car and I search around for Dad, but I don't see him anywhere. I don't see anyone who looks like a diva either.

I glance back at Mom. Her eyes look far away as she takes in all the families too. Then she shifts her purse to her shoulder and straightens her blazer. "Chop-chop, Wren," she says, taking my hand. "Time to meet your teacher."

Ms. Little is standing just outside our coat-room door, greeting everyone as Mom and I walk down the hallway. A bunch of people, including Amber and her family, are crowded around her, so I can't see exactly what she looks like. But I catch a glimpse of short, brownish hair, and a bubble-gum-pink blouse. As we get closer, I can see that Phoebe and Eleanor aren't here yet, but Bowtie, Noah, and another boy, Mitchell, are there. They are standing still and smiling sweetly, which is total make-believe from how they usually act. I crane my neck, looking up and down the hall. Still no Dad.

"He's probably just running late," Mom says, giving me a sideways glance. Sometimes she knows what I'm thinking without me saying a word. "You know how he loves to talk on and on with people."

Dad is a building contractor, which means he fixes lots of houses. Almost everyone in town knows him. He's always waving at people from his truck, or stopping at the café to chat with them over coffee. The way Mom says it, though, makes me wonder if Dad will be here at all. The lawyers decided Mom would be in charge of me during the week. Dad is in charge of me on the weekends. It's Tuesday today, so Mom is in charge. Maybe it's against the rules for Dad to see me?

I'm just about to text him to say I don't care about the rules, and I want him to come, when Mom shoos my phone away and pulls me toward my new teacher. "Hello, Ms. Little, I'm Emily Byrd," Mom says as they shake hands. "Wren's mom."

"It's very nice to meet you, Mrs. Byrd!" Ms. Little says cheerfully.

She must not know about the divorce. I look at my mom.

"It's very nice to meet you too," Mom replies.

Ms. Little doesn't know. And Mom didn't tell her.

Ms. Little smiles at me. "Welcome, Wren! I'm so happy you're in my class. We'll do big things this year!" She smiles again, which makes her pretty pink cheeks go up and her green eyes crinkle and the teeny diamond on her eyebrow sparkle. Her nail polish sparkles too. So do her shiny bubble-gum-pink shoes.

School hasn't even started yet and already my

teacher sparkles. I smile back at her. "Is that a real diamond?" I ask, looking at her eyebrow again.

Mom tenses next to me. "Wren," she says, like my question is silly.

I duck my eyes. But Ms. Little just laughs lightly. "No, it's not real," she tells me, "but your question makes me wonder where real diamonds come from. We'll have to look that up sometime, Wren."

"Hey, Squirt!" a familiar voice calls out.

I turn like a flash and see Dad walking toward us.

"Dad!" I shout, running to meet him even though it's against the rules to run in the hallways, and even though I've told him a million times *not* to call me Squirt in public anymore. But right now, I don't care about school rules or babyish nicknames. All I care about is seeing him.

I jump into his arms like a kindergartener. He gives my cheek a whisker rub. "I didn't think you'd come!" I say, hugging his neck.

"What?" Dad says. "I wouldn't miss your big day for the world." He hitches me up a notch higher. "Uff! Did you eat rocks for supper?"

I giggle. "I had pizza. What did you have?"

"Same same!" Dad says. "We're two peas in a pod."

I smile and hug his neck again. It smells like sawdust and soap. My favorite smell.

As Dad sets me down, he leans in and squints one eye like he does when he's going to joke around. "So what do we think of your new teacher?" He looks down the hallway, eyeing Ms. Little suspiciously. "Is she a keeper, or do I have to have a talk with the principal?"

I giggle again and shake my head. "She's nice. I like her."

I take his hand and introduce him to Ms. Little. Then I watch as he and Mom stand side by side, talking with my teacher about boring school stuff, like lunch money, student activity cards, and bus routes.

If you didn't know it, you'd think he never left.

CHAPTER 3

★

What Do Lies Taste Like?

As Mom and Dad chat with the other parents, I get ready to decorate the paper person Ms. Little gave to me a few minutes ago. She gave one to Amber too, after we had cookies and punch at the snack table. Well, *I* had cookies and punch. Amber was busy texting that new girl, Marianna.

Now we're going through the art supplies Ms. Little gave us at a bean-shaped table at the back of our classroom, along with Bo, Ty, Mitchell, and Noah. Mitchell and Noah peel the labels off the crayons. Bo and Ty stick markers under their lips, like walrus tusks. They flap their arms like flippers and grunt at Amber and me. "Grrrugh! . . . ugh . . . ugh!" which, I'm sure, is walrus talk for, "Look at us! Aren't we funny?" Typical Bowtie behavior.

Grabbing a few markers, I look at my paper person. It doesn't have a face or hair or even *clothes* yet. Ms. Little told me to decorate it to look like me, and I, Wren Jo Byrd, am nine years old. Four feet tall. Not very wide.

I get busy. Peach crayon for my skin. Brown marker for my hair. Dark blue for my eyes. Light blue for my jeans. Pink shirt. Orange sneakers.

"Darn, she's gone," Amber mutters, setting down her phone. She picks up a crayon and draws a frowny face on her paper person. "Is this school-work? Because school doesn't start for *Two Whole Days.*"

"Think of it as *fun*work," I say, happy that she's at least talking to me. Before this summer, we talked all the time. If we weren't together at her house, or my house, or at school, we were talking on the phone.

Amber mumbles something I can't hear, picks

up another crayon, and draws brown waves for her hair. "So why didn't you?" she asks, slanting her eyes at me.

"Why didn't I what?" I ask.

"Answer my texts this summer," she says. "Or send one to me? That's what phones are for, you know."

I glance around the table. The boys are busy laughing at each other's paper people. The grown-ups are talking. I could tell Amber the truth right now. That it was the worst summer of my life and that I was afraid if I called her in the middle of it, I'd start crying and never be able to stop.

"*Fine,* if you don't want to tell me, *don't.*" Amber goes back to coloring hard on her paper person.

"Nice work, girls." Mom walks up to us with a cup of coffee in her hand.

Amber glances up. "Thanks, Mrs. Byrd," she mumbles.

Bo and Ty look up too, markers still sticking out of their mouths like walrus tusks. "Gugh? Ugh, ugh?" They hold up their paper people for Mom to see.

Mom studies their paper people. "Your work is . . . interesting, boys," she says. "If you actually had tentacles, instead of arms, I'd say you've drawn them perfectly."

Bo and Ty give Mom tusky grins. "Shank you, Mishush Myrd!" they reply before spitting out their markers.

Mom just smiles and sips her coffee. The boys think Mom is still *Mrs.* Byrd, just like Amber and Ms. Little. I'm the only one who knows the truth.

Mom wanders away. I go back to work on my paper person, but all the while I'm stretching my neck, sneaking looks at my parents. *Are they talking to each other? Is that Dad's laugh I hear? Is he telling Mom a funny story? Is she laughing too?*

Stretch . . .

Stretch . . .

S t r e t c h . . .

My neck feels like it belongs on a rubber chicken, but I have to know if my parents are acting like we are still a family.

Dad is leaning against the classroom sink, sipping punch and talking with Amber's dad. He glances up when Mom walks by, but she doesn't stop. She doesn't even say *hi* with her eyes, which makes my belly button tighten like a screw.

Mom pauses at the edge of a conversation some of the other moms are having. As more families arrive, she slips back to the snack table and adds creamer to her coffee. She stirs it in slowly.

Ruby Olson takes off her jacket, drops it on a desk, and heads over to the snack table too.

"Did you have a nice summer, Ruby?" Mom asks as she pours her a cup of punch.

"It was okay," Ruby replies, taking the cup from Mom. "Did you?"

"Y-yes," Mom says. "Yes we did. A very nice summer." She gives Ruby a firm smile, then starts straightening up the cookie tray.

Ruby nabs one, then goes back to her family.

"That's a lie," Amber suddenly says. She's pointing at Mitchell's paper person. "Aliens don't have zombie eyes. Everyone knows zombies are human."

"Spoken like a true zombie," Mitchell replies, adding more swirls to his paper alien's big round eyes.

Amber squints.

"Done," Bo says, pushing back from the table. His paper person has a beard and devil horns now.

"I'm done too," Ty says, putting the final touches on his person's fangs. Noah's person has an eye patch and a peg leg. Mitchell's has pointy ears. Instead of dark brown skin, he drew it bright green.

"Ms. Little is going to make you do them over," I tell the boys. "They're supposed to look like you."

"What do you care, Byrd?" Bo asks.

"Yeah, what do you care, *Byrd*brain?" Ty adds, aping Bo.

They both snicker, but soon stop when a sudden shriek makes us all look across the room. Ruby Olson is standing in a red puddle. Punch is dripping from her fingers and splattered, like a fireworks display, across her white shirt. A girl I've never seen before is butting through the crowd, headed for the snack table, her long hair pulled back in a tight ponytail. It swings above her skinny shoulders. I read the big, sparkly word that's printed across her cute purple shirt: *Seattle*.

Amber gasps. "Marianna!"

Ruby grabs Marianna by the shoulder. "Hey! Watch what you're doing!" she shouts.

Marianna turns toward Ruby. *"Oh. Em. Gee!"* she exclaims, gawking at the red punch soaking into Ruby's shirt. "You didn't get any on *me,* did you? My outfit is *Brand. New!"*

Marianna checks herself over.

Ruby narrows her eyes. *"You're* the one who made me spill!"

"Say now, Marianna." A super-tall man rushes up to them. He makes Marianna look extra-shrimpy. "Tell your new friend you're sorry."

Marianna squints at him. "It's not *my* fault." She points at Ruby. *"She* was blocking the snacks!"

"We're awfully sorry," the tall man says to Mrs. Olson as she gives Ruby a napkin to wipe off her drippy fingers. He pulls a wallet from his back pocket. "Let me pay for her shirt."

Mrs. Olson shoos the man's money away. "Not necessary," she says. "It's just an old hand-me-down. No harm done."

Ms. Little hurries over from the sink and starts dabbing at Ruby's shirt with soggy paper towels.

"It's not so bad," she tells Ruby, even though it's not true. "I'm sure it will wash out."

Mom offers Ruby a fresh cup of punch, but Ruby shakes her head. Then she grabs her jacket and zips it to her chin.

Marianna takes the punch from Mom instead.

Ms. Little puts on a cheerful smile as she gives Ruby and Marianna their paper people to decorate and leads them to our table. "Boys and girls, I'm sure you all know Ruby, and this is Marianna Van Den Heuval. She's new, like me."

"Van Den *Whoville*?" Bo says. He and Ty exchange smirks. Then they start mumble-singing the Dr. Seuss Whoville theme song. *"Fah who foraze, dah who doraze . . ."*

Marianna narrows her eyes.

Ruby walks around the table and sits as far away from Marianna as possible. She picks up a marker and hunches over her paper person.

Amber scoots down a chair to make room for Marianna, who sits between us. Then they launch into a huge conversation even though they've been texting each other all evening.

But as soon as Ms. Little goes back to our parents, Marianna stops talking and zeroes in on Bo and Ty. They're swaying back and forth, singing the Whoville song along with the other boys, so they don't see her snatch up a black marker. Then she leans across the table and makes a big scribble on Bo's paper person.

Bo stops singing and gapes at Marianna. "Dude!"

All the boys look.

Marianna holds the marker like a dagger. "*Don't* make fun of my name," she says.

Ty gulps and pulls his paper person away. So do Mitchell and Noah.

Amber stares at Marianna for a moment. Then she smiles and gives her a high five.

Even though Bo totally deserved to get scribbled, I'm shocked by Marianna's boldness. Especially considering she's been a student at Oak Hill Elementary for approximately seven minutes. "Scribbling on other people's work really isn't allowed here," I say to her, after she sets down the black marker.

Marianna raises her eyebrows a notch higher

and purses her glossy lips. "What *I* don't allow is childish behavior."

I frown. "I'm just saying, you'll get in trouble with the teacher if you keep doing stuff like that."

Amber gives me a sharp look.

Ruby glances up.

Marianna lifts her chin slowly, as if she's wearing a crown. "Who *are* you, anyway?" she asks me.

"I'm Wren," I reply. "Wren Jo Byrd."

Marianna sniffs a laugh. "You're *fibbing,* right? Tell me the truth. What's your real name?"

"I *am* telling you the truth!"

"Huh," Marianna says. "Don't take this the wrong way, but your name sounds like a cartoon. You know, Wren *Bird*? Bugs *Bunny*? *Sponge* Bob?" Her eyes brighten. "I know . . . I'll call you *Tweety*!"

"Tweety *Byrd*," Bo says, snickering. "Good one."

"Yeah, good one," Ty adds, flapping his wings.

Marianna smiles at Bowtie. "I'm always coming up with clever nicknames for my friends," she chirps.

"*My* friends don't call people names," I say,

looking at Amber again. She knows I'm right. But she doesn't back me up. She just scoots closer to Marianna. "What's *my* nickname?" she asks.

Marianna thinks for a moment. "I'll call you *Am*," she says. "And you can call me *Em*. Get it? *Am 'n' Em?* Like the candy!"

"Sweet!" Amber says. They do another high five.

By the time Phoebe and Eleanor arrive, the boys have gone back to adding more details to their paper people. Bo even changes Marianna's scribble into a jagged scar, which all the guys think is uber-cool. They beg Marianna to scribble on their paper people too. She happily complies as Phoebe and Eleanor squeeze in around our table, saying hi to Amber and Marianna. They must have met her at the pool this summer.

But I haven't seen Phoebe and Eleanor since the day I left. Normally, I'd want to catch up with them, but nothing is normal here.

"Where were you all summer, Wren?" Phoebe asks. "I was *devastated* you missed my cookout!"

Amber looks over from gossiping with Marianna. "That's nothing. She missed *my* birthday."

Eleanor gasps. "I forgot about that! Were you sick?"

"No . . . um . . . I was visiting my grandparents, that's all," I say.

Phoebe blinks behind her glasses. "For the *whole* summer?"

My skin prickles like ants are crawling over me. "No, not for the *whole* summer. I mean, I was there at first, but . . . then . . . my parents . . . took me on a trip." I scratch my leg. My mouth tastes like pennies.

Amber cuts out of her conversation with Marianna again. She squints at me. "You went on a *trip*? Thanks for the postcard."

"Where did you go?" Eleanor asks.

I bite my lip, thinking. "Mount Rushmore?" It's not a total lie. We did go there once, when I was little.

"I've never been to Mount Rushmore," Eleanor says. "Was it cool?"

I shrug, trying to remember what it was like. "It was okay. I mean, it's just a big rock, you know? It's not like those guys do anything."

"We went panning for gold when I was there," Phoebe puts in. "My brother and I both found some. Just little flakes, but we got to keep them for a souvenir." Phoebe looks at me. "Did you find any gold while you were there?"

"Um . . . no," I reply. "Just . . . rocks . . . and things."

Marianna sniffs. "You should have gone to Seattle. There's tons of cool stuff to do there."

"Is that where you went on your vacation?" Eleanor asks Marianna.

"I'm *from* Seattle." Marianna does a diva pose, showing off her sparkly shirt.

"Oops," Eleanor says. "That's right, I forgot."

But Marianna is too busy talking about how great Seattle is to hear Eleanor's apology. She's talking loud, but I don't really hear what she's saying. The girls believed me when I said we went on a family vacation. Not even Amber could tell I was fibbing. The boys and Ruby heard me say it too. So far, I haven't had to tell the truth about this summer to anyone.

On the way home later, I ask Mom what the difference is between a fib and a lie.

"Look it up," she replies.

Fib
- An untrue statement about something small and unimportant
- A harmless lie

Lie
- To intentionally create an untrue statement
- To mislead
- To fabricate the truth

Then I look up the word *fabricate*.

Fabricate
- To build something
- To make up a false story

"So what did you learn?" Mom asks as I put my phone away.

"Fibs are little. They don't hurt anyone," I reply. "Lies are bigger. They take more work."

"That seems accurate," Mom replies. She pulls into our driveway and turns off the car. "Brush your teeth, then off to bed."

"But it's only nine o'clock," I say. "I still have another day of summer vacation."

"We need to start our new schedule now," Mom replies. "Bedtime is at nine. I have to work tomorrow morning, so you'll be coming to the library with me."

"What about Dad?" I ask, unbuckling my seat belt. "Maybe he has tomorrow off."

"Tomorrow is *Wednesday,* Wren," Mom says, getting out of the car. "Check the schedule. You're with me."

CHAPTER 4

★

What's a Reuben?

I was hoping to spend my last day of summer vacation with Amber, Phoebe, and Eleanor, but now that they believe nothing weird is going on with my family, I don't want to mess things up. If I ask them to meet me at the library, Mom might say something to give away my secret. If I bike to the park with them, or we meet up at Large Marge's for ice cream, they might ask more questions that are hard to answer. Then I'll have to think up more lies. It's better to hang out alone.

While Mom gets the library in order the next morning, I start building a book nook out of chairs and carts. *Book nook* is what G-ma called the little shelters I built when I was staying at her house this summer. She let me drape blankets over tables and chairs, then I'd crawl inside and read books, or draw pictures, or just lie there with my eyes closed, and pretend it was a boat, or a cave, or a spaceship that could fly a million light-years away. Anything could happen. Storms. Creepy bug invasions. Alien attacks. But one thing never changed. I was always the girl who saved the day. Mom said I can build a book nook here as long as the library isn't busy.

I settle in, pulling books and art supplies from my backpack. Just as I open my sketchpad to a blank page, the library's front door opens. I look up, hoping to see Dad walk in. He's always hanging around town, getting supplies or meeting with people who have broken windows and leaky roofs.

But it's not Dad.

It's that new girl. Marianna Van Den *Whoville*.

She pauses in the doorway and adjusts the tote bag that's hanging from her elbow. "Oh. Em. *Gee,*" she says as she looks the place over. Based on the way she wrinkles up her nose, I'm guessing she isn't impressed with the Oak Hill Public Library.

Good. Maybe she won't stick around.

I duck down in my book nook, watching as she marches up to Mom's desk, tote bag swinging. She rings the little bell, even though Mom is sitting right there. "Excuse me," she says, tapping the bell again. "*I* am Marianna Van Den Heuval, and I would like to purchase a library card."

Mom stops typing and looks up from her computer. "Good morning, Marianna Van Den Heuval," she replies, propping her glasses on top of her head. "Welcome to the Oak Hill Public Library. I'm afraid we don't sell library cards here."

Marianna blinks. "What do you mean? I have plenty of money." She opens her tote bag and pulls out a beaded coin purse. "If this isn't enough, I can get more."

She unzips the coin purse and pulls out a wad of crumpled bills. "You don't understand, Marianna," Mom says. "Library cards are *free*."

Marianna crinkles her eyebrows. "*Free?* For reals?"

"I'm quite serious," Mom says, opening a desk drawer. "All I need is a parent's signature." She takes out a form and looks toward the library entrance. "Are your parents here?"

Marianna shakes her head. "My parents are in Seattle. My stepdad is in charge of me until my mother gets here. We just moved into the ginormous house around the corner. The one that's as big as a castle? I'm sure you've seen it. It's got a cul-de-sac and everything. Do you know what *cul-de-sac* means? It's French for circle."

"How nice," Mom replies. "Take this form home and ask your stepfather to sign it. You'll have to wait until he returns it to me, before you may check out books."

"But I need a book about orcas *now*. I'm going to surprise my teacher with a book report on the first day of school, which, in case you haven't heard, is *tomorrow?*" She lifts her tote bag and shows Mom a black-and-white whale printed on it. "Orcas are my best subject. But all my books are still in boxes, so I have to get one *here*."

Mom smiles patiently. Then she calmly explains

the rules about permission forms, and using our quiet voices in the library. She puts on her glasses again and brings up a new screen on her computer. "We have several books on orcas . . ."

While Mom searches the library's catalog, and Marianna waits, I think about her plan to write a book report for the first day of school. Ms. Little might give Marianna extra credit for an unassigned book report. She might even tack the report to the blue bulletin board by her desk. I noticed it at Family Night. The words *We're Up to Something Big!* were stapled across the top of it. Ms. Little might even nominate Marianna for Oak Hill Elementary's Student of the Week! I've been nominated for Student of the Week four times so far, but *never* on the first day of school.

". . . and here's a happy coincidence," Mom says, her crisp librarian voice skipping past Marianna's wooden frown. "Wren is here too."

"What's a *wren*?"

"Wren is my daughter," Mom replies, looking toward me.

I sink down.

But Marianna sees me anyway. "Oh," she says, her voice as dull as safety scissors. "It's *you* again. Hello, *Tweety*."

I paste on a fake-friendly smile. "Hello, Mar-*iguana*," I reply.

Marianna's eyes flash at me.

So do Mom's. She stands up, straightens her blazer, then steps out from behind her desk. "I'll find a selection of orca books for you, Marianna," she says, nudging her toward me. "You may read them here." Then she disappears between the bookshelves.

Marianna stuffs her money back inside her tote bag. She gives my book nook the once-over. "What's this supposed to be? Your playhouse?"

"No," I reply. "It's called a *book nook*."

Marianna sniffs, unimpressed. She looks at the pile of chapter books sitting next to me. At my sketchpad. At the pens and markers scattered around. *Sniff-sniff-sniff.*

Maybe she has allergies. I hope she's allergic to me.

She picks up my sketchpad and flips through

a few pages before tossing it aside again. "I draw too," she says, moving a book cart and sitting down across from me. "My mother is a *real* artist. As soon as she finishes her last big project in Seattle, she's moving here with Reuben and me. It will be any day now."

"What's a reuben?" I ask.

Marianna purses her lips. "Reuben is my stepdad."

"Oh," I say. "I thought it was a sandwich."

Marianna rolls her eyes at my joke, then takes one of my purple gel pens and starts doodling on her hand. "He and my mom got married this spring. Are your parents still married?"

I stiffen.

Marianna looks up.

"Mmm-hmm," I say, which feels like a smaller lie than *Yes*.

"My parents got divorced ages ago," Marianna says, going back to her doodle. She blows on the purple ink, then switches to orange.

I stretch my neck, trying to see the design that's taking shape on her hand. It looks like two tadpoles—one purple, one orange—curled up together inside a circle. But they don't look like real tadpoles, which are a muddy brown color and shaped like a blob. Her tadpoles are more like commas in a story. She's really good at decorating them with tiny swirls and delicate curlicues, like lace, or window frost in the winter.

"It's called yin-yang," Marianna says, glancing up.

I sit back.

"Ever heard of it?"

"No," I say truthfully.

Marianna sniffs. "I didn't think so. No offense, but you don't seem like the kind of girl who would know much about balance and wholeness and stuff. My friends and I draw yin-yang all the time." She drops the gel pen and leans against a book cart, stretching out her legs. "I have *five* best friends in Seattle. How many do you have?"

"Just one," I reply. "Amber."

Marianna sits up again. "For reals? *Am* is your *BFF*?"

"Yes," I reply, even though it doesn't feel exactly

true. Since getting back home, everything feels different with my family and with Amber. "We've been best friends forever."

"Huh. Weird."

"Why is that weird?"

Marianna shrugs. "It's just, Am didn't say anything about you being best friends. Where I come from, that's the first thing we tell people. What about that other girl? The one who almost spilled punch on me."

"Ruby Olson? She's just in my class."

Marianna frowns. "Huh. Weird," she says again.

"Now what?" I ask.

"Calm down, Tweety," Marianna says. "It's just, if I had to friend you with someone, it would be Ruby Red Punch, not Am."

The way Marianna says it makes my arm hairs bristle. We only met yesterday. She doesn't know anything about me or my friends. "No offense, but the French word for circle is *cercle,* not *cul-de-sac.*"

Marianna narrows her eyes. "How would *you* know?"

"I read books," I say. "Have you ever read an *actual* book?"

Her nostrils flare. She flicks back her ponytail. "I was the *best* reader at my old school."

I smile. "The best reader at your new school is *me*."

Marianna smirks. "Prove it."

"I won the Old Hill Public Library reading trophy two summers in a row. I would have won this summer too, if I hadn't had to stay with my grandpar—if I hadn't gone on vacation."

Marianna barks a laugh. "Of course you won! Your *mother* is the librarian."

I squint. "I won fair and square."

Marianna sniffs.

Mom returns with a bunch of books in the crook of her arm. She crouches down, showing them to Marianna. "This one has exceptional photographs," Mom says, holding out a picture book about whales to Marianna.

Marianna purses her lips like a sea turtle. "I read *novels* now."

Mom nudges the picture book into Marianna's hands. "Big things come in small packages," she tells her. It makes me think of the last time Amber and I played birthday party. We wrapped up presents for each other in little boxes. Amber gave me her best bracelet. The one she made out of bright blue gum wrappers. I wore it every day until it finally fell apart. And I gave her my favorite eraser—a little bird that was just as blue as the bracelet. I wonder if she still has it.

Mom talks on and on about each book, but all I can think about is what Marianna said earlier.

- Amber didn't tell her we are best friends.
- Reuben is her stepdad.
- Her parents are divorced too.

I'm not the only one.

"I'll get that form for you to bring home," Mom says, standing up again. "If your stepfather could drop it off later today, that would be convenient. I need to speak with him about something."

Marianna nods, paging through one of the books.

Mom heads back to her desk.

I hurry after her.

"Why do you need to talk to Marianna's step-dad?" I ask in a low voice. "Are you going to warn him about the stinkbugs crawling out of her ears?"

Mom makes a face. "Very funny. I'm going to ask him if Marianna can walk here with you after school. I'd feel better knowing you're walking here with a friend. Her house is just around the corner."

My eyes go wide. "That girl is *not* my friend, Mom."

"She's in your class," Mom says, picking up the form from her desk. "You both have two functioning legs. She can be your friend for ten minutes every Monday through Thursday from three thirty to three forty p.m."

"But that's why you and Dad gave me a phone!" I shout.

Marianna glances over. I swallow down the loudness in my voice and start again. "Oak Hill isn't big, Mom. I can go places *By. My. Self!*"

Mom smiles in a *this-conversation-is-over* way.

Then she hands the form to me. "Please give this to Marianna. Quietly."

I give Mom the stink eye. But I take the form from her.

Marianna is rearranging my book nook as I trudge back to her. Turning chairs and moving carts. "There, that's better," she says, stretching out her legs again. "Sit down, Tweety." She picks up my sketchpad and a pen. "I'll teach you how to do *real* art."

I grip the form until it crumples.

Mom can make me walk here with that girl, I say to myself. *But she can't make me be her friend.*

CHAPTER 5

★

But Why?!

Mom is at the kitchen counter, reading the newspaper and drinking her coffee, when I come downstairs for breakfast the next morning. I'm still mad about what happened at the library yesterday. After Mom lied and told Marianna that I would *love* to walk to the library with her after school, Marianna texted her stepdad, Reuben. He came right over to sign the library permission form and to tell Mom he was totally in favor of her plan, and that he was so happy Marianna had made "another new friend" in Oak Hill.

Then Marianna patted my shoulder and said,

"Don't worry, Mrs. Byrd, I'll make sure your daughter gets here safely."

Grrrugh.

While Mom and Reuben talked, Marianna pulled me away, bragging about how she can read a whole chapter book in *Only. One. Day.* And how she can do five backflips in a row, and that she has seen *actual orcas* in the wild. Then she stuffed my head with orca facts *(Did you know, Tweety, orcas are a kind of dolphin . . . ? They hunt in packs like wolves . . . ? Their brains weigh almost as much as a watermelon . . . ?)*

By the time she and her stepdad left, my head felt as big as a watermelon.

Mom looks up from her newspaper. "Happy first day of school!" she says cheerfully, like she can't see the frown on my face. "I got a box of that special fruity cereal you like."

"I don't like that kind anymore," I grumble. "Dad always makes chocolate chip pancakes and bacon for breakfast on my first day of school."

"Oh," Mom says. She clears her throat. "I forgot about that." She sets down her newspaper. "I'll make pancakes tomorrow morning. Blueberry. They're healthier than chocolate chip."

"Never mind," I say, taking a box of granola from the cupboard.

I pour the granola into a bowl Mom sets on the counter, add some milk, and start chewing.

"You should add more milk," Mom says, watching me eat. "Then it wouldn't be so hard to chew."

I scoop another spoonful into my mouth.

Mom sips her coffee, studying me with a slight frown on her face.

"What?" I finally ask.

"I was just looking at your outfit," Mom replies. "I like the skirt you chose, but that shirt has a stain. When you're finished with breakfast, please change your top and put that one in the laundry."

I swallow. "But this is my new favorite shirt! I want to wear it for my first day."

"Wear the one with the elephant pattern," Mom says, picking up her newspaper again. "Elephants are just as good as giraffes."

I grip my spoon like a cave girl and shovel in another scoop.

The kitchen is silent, except for the crunching in my mouth and the rustling of Mom's newspaper. She keeps turning pages, like she's reading the articles, but her eyes are flitting from column to column, like they don't know where to land.

A minute later, she closes the newspaper and looks at me. "I really am very sorry I forgot about the pancakes," she says quietly. "Why don't we play that question game you and your dad like so much?"

"It's not a game," I tell her. It's just something Dad started doing when I was little. We used to do it all the time—in the car, at supper, before bedtime. Sometimes I would ask the questions, but I liked it best when Dad did because he mixed them all together—funny, serious, goofy—you never knew what was coming next. It's one of my favorite things, but we haven't played it for a long time.

"Okay," Mom says. "But can I ask some?"

Crunch . . . crunch . . . "Fine." *. . . crunch . . .*

Mom thinks for a moment. "Do you know what day of the week it is?"

I roll my eyes. "Thursday."

"Correct. And what happens after school on Thursdays?"

"I have to walk to the library."

"Good! And who will you be walking with?"

"Mar-*iguana* Van Den *Whoville*."

Mom purses her lips. "Wren, please don't call people names. It's childish."

"But she calls me Tweety!" I complain.

"Two wrongs don't make a right. Now let me think . . . What is the capital of Kentucky?"

"I don't know. Why can't G-ma come stay with me after school instead?"

"Frankfort. Your grandmother lives too far away. Who was the fourteenth president of the United States?"

I sigh. "Abraham Lincoln? Why can't Dad watch me after school? He always used to. Or what about Aunt Claire? She lives close by. I could even ride my bike to her house."

"Abraham Lincoln was our *sixteenth* president. Franklin Pierce was fourteenth. You're my responsibility during the week now. And that would be asking too much of Aunt Claire."

"Why?!" I protest. "I used to go over to her house all the time. We all did. You. Me. Dad."

"Things are different now, Wren. Aunt Claire is your dad's sister. It's awkward for me to be there."

"But why?!"

"We'll talk about it later," she says. But I know we won't. She never wants to talk about the big things. "For now, stick to our plan." She taps the schedule on the refrigerator door. I notice the smiley face magnet is turned right side up again.

"*Your* plan." I let my spoon fall into my cereal bowl. *Thunk!*

"You ask *me* a question now," Mom says, coming back to the counter. "Something silly . . . or funny."

"But that's not how it works. Dad asks me twenty questions before it's my turn."

"Well, this is how I play the game," Mom replies. "Ask me a question."

I push my bowl away and cross my arms. "How come you and Dad got a divorce?"

Mom's jaw tightens. Her fingers twitch on her coffee cup. "That is a big question for another time, Wren," she replies. "Also, technically, we're not divorced yet, just separated."

I straighten up. "What does that mean? You and Dad are still married?? Then how come he had to move out???"

"We're not married," Mom replies. "At least, not in the way you think. Separation is an . . . in-between time. It's not the same as being married."

"But it's not the same as being divorced either, right?"

"I suppose that's true. Now, ask me a different question. Something more creative."

"Do people who are separated *have* to get divorced?" I ask.

Mom sighs. She checks her watch. "No, I don't suppose they *have* to. But they *do*. Your dad and I *are*. Now, chop-chop. Go brush your teeth and change your shirt. I don't want you to be late for your first day of school."

Mom carries my cereal bowl and her coffee cup to the sink.

Game over.

*   *   *

After I change clothes, I look up the word *separation*.

Separation
• An arrangement by which a husband and wife live apart
• Break
• Division
• Gap

"I was right," I say, looking over at Shakespeare. He's watching from my bedroom windowsill. "They are still husband and wife."

"Mew?" Shakespeare says, flicking his tail.

I nod. "Separation is different than divorce. They can still get back together."

CHAPTER 6

★

Can They Tell I Have Two Bedrooms Now?

Mom drops me off at school on her way to the library. Amber's mom pulls up beside us in the parking lot and gives us a friendly wave. She lowers her window to talk to Mom as Amber, Ivory, and Slate get out of their van.

But Mom keeps her window up. She taps her watch and mouths the words *running late* to Mrs. Lane. Then she turns to me. "Hurry now, Wren. I need to go. See you after school. Don't forget to—"

"Walk with Marianna," I cut in. "I know, Mom. You don't have to remind me."

Mom smiles. "I'm pleased you've memorized the schedule. Now, chop-chop. Have a good day."

I climb out of the car. Mom zooms away.

"Hello, Wren!" Mrs. Lane calls to me from her van.

"Hi, Mrs. Lane," I reply, walking up to her window.

"I was hoping to chat with your mom," she says. "We barely had a chance to talk at Family Night. We haven't seen your family in ages! How is everything?"

"Everything is fine," I reply.

"Did you have a nice summer vaca—"

"Are you *deaf* or something?" Amber comes around the side of the van with her big sister breathing down her neck. Slate is on their heels.

Amber and Ivory are always fighting about something. Sometimes I wish I had a big sister, and sometimes I'm glad I don't.

"What is it today?" I ask Slate as he slides over to my side. "Let me guess, Ivory was hogging the bathroom again? Or maybe Amber ate the last toaster tart?"

Slate shakes his head. "Amber is wearing one of Ivory's necklaces."

"Oooo . . ." I say. "Deadly."

Slate nods mournfully.

"I *told* you, Ivory, I thought the necklace was mine!" Amber shoves her sister away.

"Liar!" Ivory shouts. "You knew it was mine! Now give it back!" She lunges for Amber's throat.

Amber squirms and kicks. "I'll give it to you after school!" she wails.

"Give it to me *now*!"

"No!"

"Yes!"

"Girls!" Mrs. Lane leans out of the van and shoots dagger eyes at Amber and Ivory. "Stop *shouting*!" she shouts. "Ivory, leave your sister alone. Amber, take off that necklace this minute."

"But . . . !" Amber protests.

"No *but*s," Mrs. Lane says. "Give the necklace back to Ivory. Take Slate to his classroom. Now!"

Amber snarls and claws at the clasp.

Ivory lets go of Amber and holds out her hand.

Amber throws the necklace on the ground

instead. "I hope you're happy!" she screams at her sister. "Now my neck is completely naked!"

"Not my problem," Ivory says calmly, picking up the necklace and putting it on. Then she pops in her ear buds, gives Slate a high five, and walks across the parking lot toward the middle school.

Angry tears spring to Amber's eyes. She crosses her arms over her chest, chin quivering.

"Here, take this," I say, pulling a jelly bracelet off my wrist. "At least your arm won't be naked. Plus it's purple! Your favorite color." I do my best BFF smile.

Amber sighs and, reluctantly, takes the jelly from me. "Thanks," she grumbles, slipping it on. "Purple is Em's favorite color too."

"Em?" I say.

"Marianna?" Amber replies.

"Oh," I say. "Her."

Amber grabs Slate by the hand, then scowls at her mother.

"Bye, love," Mrs. Lane says. "Have a good day, Wren! Slate, I'll see you after school."

"Bye, Mommy! Look, Wren! That's my new

school!" Slate shouts as Amber yanks him toward the entrance.

I hurry to catch up. "Speaking of Marianna, I saw her at the library yesterday. Now I have to walk there with her after school."

Amber stops and gawks at me. "You get to walk with Em? *No. Fair!*"

"It's not like I want to," I say. "My mom is making me. How come you haven't told Marianna that I'm your best—"

"Am!" someone shouts. "Tweety! Over here!"

We look down the sidewalk and see Marianna waving wildly. Amber pushes Slate toward me. "Walk him to class for me, *pleeease,* Wren?" she pleads. "You don't like Em anyway, and I've *got* to talk to her!"

"But . . ." I say, looking at Slate. "Don't you want your sister to walk with you?"

Slate shakes his head. "I don't want *nobody* to walk with me! I'm *big*!"

Slate takes off for the main doors. Amber flies down the sidewalk to Marianna. I just stand there in the middle of nowhere, kids bumping past me, talking, laughing, excited for their first day of school.

By the time I get to our coatroom, Amber and Marianna are linked up, chattering like chipmunks about their new school supplies and cute outfits and sparkly shoes. Amber is gaga over the necklace Marianna is wearing—a thin silver chain with a milky blue pendant.

"Where did you get it?" Amber asks as Marianna twirls the pendant. At first I think it's a stone, but now it looks more like glass.

"My mother made it," Marianna replies. "She makes lots of jewelry. She made my barrette too, see?" She turns around so Amber can admire the fancy barrette that's holding back Marianna's long hair. It's shaped like a butterfly. The wings are painted with swirls and curlicues, just like that yin-yang thing she was drawing yesterday at the library.

"Do my hair like yours!" Amber begs.

"Okay," Marianna agrees. "But you'll need a barrette."

Amber slumps. "I didn't bring any." In a flash, she turns to me. "Wren, let me borrow a barrette." She holds out her hand, knowing I'll have one in my backpack. My mom always packs extra hair clips in the zipper pocket.

Unzipping the pocket, I pull out two clips. Amber snatches them from my hand and pulls Marianna out the door.

"You're welcome," I say. But they're already at the girls' restroom.

I find my cubby and hang up my stuff. Other kids are coming in now too. Zach, Mitchell, Ruby, Noah, Jordan . . . I watch as they put their stuff away, some heading into our classroom, others standing around talking. Except for their trimmed hair and new school clothes, everyone looks the same as last year.

I wonder if I look the same too. Or does divorce change more than just your family? Can they tell I've got two bedrooms now? Two toothbrushes? Two sets of pajamas? Will they wonder why I turn left at the corner and walk to the library after school, instead of turning right? Will they ask why I'm

62
★ ★ ★

riding Bus #5 on Fridays? Will they look at me weird when I do?

I don't want to be weird. I want to be the same as before . . . before my parents started fighting. Before they stopped talking. Before we weren't a family anymore.

Bo races in with Ty right behind him. He dives for his cubby. "I win!" Bo shouts.

Ty collapses against the doorway, panting. "Only . . . because . . . I got . . . hung up . . . on the bus! Kindergarteners are so slow! I'll beat you tomorrow."

Bo waves off Ty and hangs up his backpack. "In your dreams."

Just then, Amber and Marianna return, with matching hairdos. Ty sees them coming and sticks out his foot. Marianna stumbles over it and falls, flat as a pancake on the shiny tile floor. Ty barks a laugh. So does Bo. Everyone in the coatroom stops talking and looks over.

Amber flies to Marianna's side. "Are you okay?" she asks, helping her up.

"Yes," Marianna says. "I'm fine."

Amber glares at Ty. "You did that on purpose!" she shouts.

Ty lifts his shoulders, playing dumb. "I didn't do anything." But he tenses up, like he expects to get punched in the arm, or kicked in the shin.

But all Marianna does is straighten her skirt and smooth down her hair. Then she cocks her head and studies Ty.

"What are you lookin' at?" Ty finally asks, twitching nervously.

"I was just wondering . . ." Marianna says thoughtfully. ". . . are *you* the boy who still wets the bed?"

Everyone gasps.

Ty's jaw drops. "Huh?" he says. "No way!"

Marianna crosses her arms and tilts her hips. "Your name is *Ty,* isn't it?" she asks. "I'm sure that's the name some kids mentioned in the hallway just now. One of them goes, 'Who's that boy who still wets the bed?' And the other one goes, 'Ty. He's in Ms. Little's class.'"

Ty's eyes bulge like Ping-Pong balls. His ears burn redder than a pair of tomatoes. "Listen,

Whoville," he says. "It ain't me!" Then he bolts for his cubby.

Everyone is practically rolling on the floor laughing as Ty shakes off his backpack and throws it onto a coat hook. "Whatcha got in there, Ty?" Bo asks, poking at Ty's backpack. "Pampers?"

Ty shoves Bo away. "Knock it off."

Everyone cracks up again.

Marianna smiles.

"Did someone really say that or is Marianna lying?" I ask Amber, under my breath.

Amber looks at me from the corners of her eyes. "So what if she is lying? It was funny. And Ty deserved it." She shifts closer to Marianna.

Phoebe and Eleanor arrive. They look at everyone huddled around Ty's cubby, making diaper jokes and dodging Ty's air jabs.

"What's going on?" they ask.

"Em started an *excellent* rumor about Ty," Amber replies.

"Why? What happened?" Phoebe asks.

Marianna shrugs. "It's no big deal. I just taught Ty a little lesson. He won't be tripping me again."

Phoebe and Eleanor exchange puzzled glances as Marianna takes a folder from the tote bag in her cubby. Then she lines us up and looks us over. "Ready to start our day, girls?" she asks.

"Ready!" Amber, Phoebe, and Eleanor reply.

Instantly, Amber links up with Marianna again. Phoebe and Eleanor toss their stuff onto coat hooks and fall in step as they parade into the classroom together.

But I lag behind. Marianna made up that story about Ty in a heartbeat. Like she's had lots of practice. I wonder what else she's lying about.

CHAPTER 7

★

How Do You Draw a Home?

Marianna comes up to me after I get into the classroom. Her desk is right behind mine. Amber's is across the room. "Your mom is the best," Marianna tells me. "I just gave Ms. Little my book report on orcas, and she was *So. Im. Pressed!* She even gave me *this.*"

Marianna holds up a mini notebook with a lavender cover. "She told me I can use it to write about moving to Oak Hill and being the new girl and stuff." She slips into her desk, thumbing through the notebook's blank pages. "I think I'll write my autobiography for her!"

I give Marianna a sideways glance. "Will it be a true story or a fable?"

Marianna looks up and scrunches her eyebrows. "What's that supposed to mean?"

"*Fable* is another word for *make-believe*," I explain.

"I know what the word means," Marianna says importantly. "But why are you asking if my story will be true or not?"

I lift my shoulder. "You're good at making things up."

Marianna pauses, like she's trying to decide if I'm dissing her, or paying her a compliment.

"Does this have anything to do with the Ty incident?" she asks. "Because that was nothing. I'm not a liar, Tweety, if that's what you're asking."

"Stop calling me that," I say. "My name is Wren, not Tweety."

Marianna takes out her pencil box and starts sifting through the gel pens inside. "I give all my friends nicknames. You can give me one too! Something that reminds you of me."

I make a face. "How about Toothache?"

Marianna smirks. "LOL, Tweety. Keep thinking."

I face forward again as Ms. Little starts taking attendance. The leopard pattern on her blouse reminds me of the costumes G-ma made for Amber and me last Halloween. We were cute little leopards. Mom and Dad dressed up like jungle explorers and took us around town. I wonder if we'll go trick-or-treating together this year. Or does divorce split up holidays too?

I could ask Marianna. She has a stepdad now, so she must know how divorced-holidays work. I wouldn't have to tell her why I want to know.

I sneak a look over my shoulder at her. She's busy writing her name in spidery letters on the cover of her new notebook. "What is it, Tweety?" she asks, not looking up. "I'm busy."

"Never mind," I mumble, and start to turn around again.

Now she looks up. "You can ask me anything," she says. "I know about lots of stuff."

I bite my lip. "It's not important, but . . . I was just wondering . . . do kids go trick-or-treating in Seattle?"

Marianna blinks. "What a silly question. Of course they do. *Everyone* goes trick-or-treating. It's a national holiday."

I shift in my chair. "What did you dress up as last year?"

Marianna sets down her pen. "A sea princess. I made the tiara myself. My mother made one too. She was the sea queen."

I turn all the way around in my chair. "Was your dad the sea king? Did you all go trick-or-treating together?"

Marianna lifts one eyebrow like an upside-down fishhook. "Why do you want to know?" she asks.

I bite my lip again. "No reason."

As Ms. Little goes over our classroom rules and daily schedule, I feel a tap on my shoulder. Marianna leans in.

"Reuben was the sea king," she whispers. "My mom made his trident. We stopped at my dad's house for candy, but he didn't go trick-or-treating with us. Does that answer your question?"

I give her a sideways nod.

"Good," she says, sitting back again.

While Ms. Little gets Amber and Mitchell to help her hand out our new textbooks, I raise my desk lid and pull up the dictionary on my phone. We're not supposed to use our phones during class, but we haven't started learning anything yet. I type in the word *trident*.

Trident
• A three-pronged spear belonging to a sea god.

There are pictures of tridents too. I scroll through them. They look like fancy pitchforks.

"You're not supposed to be texting during class," someone says.

I look up and see Amber standing next to my desk with a stack of math books.

Quickly, I turn off my phone and close my desk. "I was looking up something for school," I say. "I wasn't texting anyone."

Amber drops a book on my desk. *Thunk!* "Oh, that's right," she says. "You don't know how to text."

"Yes, I do . . . and I would have, but . . ."

She moves on to Marianna and sets a book on her desk.

"Thanks, Am!" Marianna says.

"No problem, Em!" Amber replies. They do the fancy handshake Amber and I invented last year. She must have taught it to Marianna when I was gone this summer.

After all the books have been handed out, Ms. Little picks up a stack of posters and asks Noah and me to pass them around. "I thought it would be fun to begin our year by getting to know each other a little better."

Each poster looks like a page from a coloring book, with zigzag borders to decorate and shapes to color in. *All About Me!* is printed across the top. The paper people we made at Family Night are glued to the center of each one. Noah and I match each poster to its owner, then sit down with our own. There are lots of blank spaces to fill in.

My Favorite Color!
My Favorite Food!
My Pets!
My House!
My Best Friend!

Phoebe raises her hand. "I don't have any pets, Ms. Little," she says, holding up her poster and pointing to the *My Pets!* space.

"Then draw an imaginary one!" Ms. Little replies.

Phoebe brightens. She takes a box of markers from her desk and starts drawing. I bet she's making a horse, because they are her favorite animal. Sometimes, at recess, Phoebe, Eleanor, Amber, and I pretend we have invisible horses and gallop around the playground together. At least, that's what we did last year. I wonder if they played horses over the summer too.

Opening up my pencil box, I sift through my erasers until I find an orange gel pen. I have lots of erasers because collecting them is my hobby. I have even more at home. I use the orange gel pen to write *ORANGE* in the *My Favorite Color!* space. I try to make the letters spidery, like Marianna's, but they don't turn out as good.

For my favorite food, I draw a bowl of Dad's spicy chili. The pet space is easy. I draw a white cat with a furry black goatee on his chin. *Goatee* is another word for a little beard. I looked it up once. I remember when Dad had a beard for a while, but Mom made him shave it off. She said it made him look like a hoodlum, which is another word for bad guy. I looked that one up too.

The next space is harder.

My House!

I don't have one house anymore. I have two now.

I fidget in my chair, glancing around the room. Everyone else is busy drawing. I'm the only one who doesn't know what to do.

I can't ask Ms. Little, even though she just told Ty there's no such thing as a silly question when Bo razzed him for asking if chewing gum counts as food. If I ask her my question, she'll know the truth about me. So will everyone else.

I peek over my shoulder again to see if Marianna is drawing two houses. But her poster is half-hidden in the crook of her arm and I don't want to ask her any more questions.

If I only draw one house, no one will know I'm lying, I reason.

I pick up a marker and draw Mom's house. Then I draw a bright yellow sun in the sky. I give it a smiley face. Finally, I draw Mom, Dad, me, and Shakespeare next to the house. We're all smiling too.

When I look up again, some kids are already putting their finished posters in the schoolwork basket on Ms. Little's desk. Quickly, I go back to the last blank space on my poster.

My Best Friend!

I glance across the room at Amber. She's showing her poster to Phoebe and Eleanor. Did she draw a picture of me?

Amber carries her poster to the front of the room. I watch as she sets it in the basket.

As fast as I can, I draw a picture of Amber on my poster—round face, wavy hair, rosy cheeks, friendly smile. Then I dash up to Ms. Little's desk. Before setting my poster in the basket, I look at Amber's *My Best Friend!* drawing.

It's a girl with a long ponytail and bright purple clothes.

Under her, Amber wrote two letters.

Em

"Let's play horses!" Phoebe says later, when we're all outside for recess. "We can pretend our mares had ponies over the summer!"

"Ooo . . . good idea!" Eleanor says excitedly. "Mine is black with a white mane and tail!"

Phoebe doesn't miss a beat. "Mine is light brown with a heart-shaped patch on her forehead. Her name is Valentine!"

Phoebe and Eleanor start chattering about jeweled bridles and pink saddles and braided manes.

"Wait. Stop," Marianna says, silencing Phoebe and Eleanor's jabbering. "Ponies? Horses? What are you talking about?"

"It's just a game we play," Amber explains. "See, we each have an invisible horse that we ride around on during recess."

Eleanor nods. "We make up all kinds of stories

about them. Amber and Wren have twin horses! Their names are—"

"Oh. Em. *Gee,*" Marianna cuts in. "You guys still play *pretend*?" She makes a face as we all nod. "My friends and I haven't played pretend in *For. Ev. Er.*"

"Then what do you do at recess?" I ask.

"We walk around and talk about important things," Marianna replies. "Like who can hold their breath the longest, and which lip gloss flavors taste best, and what we'll name our children when we grow up and get married."

"That sounds like fun," Amber says, even though I think it sounds dumb. "Especially the married part. Let's try it."

Marianna smiles and links elbows with Amber. "Follow me," she says, leading the way.

We stroll past the basketball court, the sandbox, the swings, and the twisty slide. Marianna stops every few minutes to tell us something important about herself.

"My dad has a big sailboat. He takes my friends and me out sailing all the time."

"My favorite seafood is crab. Salmon is good too. I've even eaten caviar! That's French for fish eggs."

"My very best friend is Sasha. You guys won't believe this, but she's even cooler than me . . ."

"And you have that huge house too!" says Amber.

"It's true. My new house is huge compared to my old house," Marianna tells us as we stop at the jungle gym. "My bedroom is so big, I could have two ginormous beds if I wanted to."

"I have two beds in my room," Amber says, "but my sister sleeps in one of them. I would give anything to have my own bedroom. Ivory drives me nuts."

"I have my own room," Phoebe says. "There's only one bed, but it does have a canopy."

"Your canopy is the coolest!" Eleanor says. "I always feel like a princess when I sleep over at your house."

Marianna sniffs. "Don't take this the wrong way, but canopy beds are kind of babyish." She looks at me. "What's your room like, Tweety? Do you have two beds?"

"No," I lie. I even have two bedrooms now.

"Too bad," Marianna says. "Still, it would be fun to see your room. You should have a sleepover! I would do it, but we're still getting unpacked because we have *So Much Stuff*."

"Ooo . . . !" Eleanor says. "A sleepover would be uber-fun! Tomorrow's Friday. Let's have one!"

"It can be our kickoff to the new school year!" Phoebe adds. "I'll bring some movies I got this summer."

"I'll make chocolate chip cookies!" Eleanor adds.

I freak out on the inside. The girls can't sleep over at my house tomorrow night! I have to stay at Dad's cabin this weekend. I've seen the cabin before because Dad drove me past it once, but I've never been inside. It's got gray siding that looks like it might have been blue at one time. The roof sags a little. And one of the front windows is missing a shutter. "But . . ." I start to say.

"It's all settled then," Marianna says. "Sleepover at Tweety's house!"

"But I can't!" I blurt out.

"Why not?" Amber asks. "Still too busy for your friends?"

"No," I say. "I mean, yes . . . I'm busy this weekend."

"Doing what?" Eleanor asks.

"Um . . ." I say, trying to think up a quick lie. "It's my dad . . . He's starting a new building project and . . . um . . . I'm helping him."

Amber makes a face. "Since when do you help your dad with his building projects?"

"Since now," I say. "He taught me how to hammer nails over the summer."

Amber rolls her eyes.

"Then we'll all come over for supper on Saturday," Phoebe says. "Ask your mom if we can make homemade pizza again! Remember how much fun that was last time? We rolled out the dough and she set out all kinds of toppings and we pretended we worked at a pizzeria!"

All the girls start gabbing about their favorite pizza toppings, until I finally shout, "Stop! You're not listening to me! I can't have a sleepover this weekend, okay?! I told you, I'm busy!"

Everyone goes quiet. I duck my head and kick at the wood chips under my feet. I wish I could dig a hole deep enough to crawl inside and disappear.

"If Wren won't have a sleepover, then I will," Amber says, breaking the silence at last. "I'll get Mom to make Ivory sleep in Slate's room. Marianna can share my bed. Phoebe and Eleanor can share Ivory's. We'll be squished, but who cares? We're not going to sleep anyway."

Phoebe and Eleanor squeal with excitement again. They start chattering, like everything is okay now.

"Bring your diaries," Amber tells them. "We'll read our secrets to each other!"

I frown at Amber. "Since when do you have a diary?" I ask.

Amber gives me a cool look. "Since my *birthday party*," she says. "You know, the one you missed?"

The recess bell rings. We start lining up to go back inside.

"Are you sure you can't come to the sleepover, Wren?" Eleanor asks as we file into the school.

"I'm sure," I mumble.

"Bummer," she says.

"It doesn't matter," I reply, even though my stomach is in knots and my eyes are stinging with tears.

CHAPTER 8

★

Why Don't Oceans Freeze?

On the sidewalk after school, I watch while Amber helps Slate get into her family's van and fastens his seat belt. Then she hops in too and starts talking with Ivory, even though they were fighting this morning. Mrs. Lane must say something funny, because Amber bursts out laughing. I miss making her laugh. How come their family gets to fight one minute, and be happy again the next?

"Here I am at last, Tweety," Marianna says as she walks up to me. "Oh, look! There goes Am!" She waves as Amber's mom pulls away from the curb.

Amber lowers her window and practically falls

out of the van, waving back to Marianna. "Bye, Emmmm!" she cries as they drive away. "See you tomorrowwwww!" She doesn't even look at me.

"It's too bad you can't come to her sleepover, Tweety," Marianna says as we start to walk along. "What does your dad build, anyway?"

"Houses, garages, decks . . . stuff like that."

"Did he build your house?" Marianna asks. She looks up and down the block. "Where do you live, anyway?"

"Not far," I reply. "My house is by the lake. My dad didn't build it."

"I know where the lake is. Let's walk by your house! You can show me your room."

"No one is at my house right now," I say. "That's why I have to go to the library. Besides, it's not on the way to Large Marge's, and we have to stop there first."

"The pizza place? Reuben and I ate there once."

I nod. "I have to buy supper."

"How come? Doesn't your mom cook either?"

"She cooks," I say. "Just not . . . lately. Her schedule changed."

"What about your dad?" Marianna persists. "Doesn't he cook?"

"Sometimes," I say. "But he's working late too." I take a breath and relax a little. The fibs are coming easier now.

"Reuben is a total cooking geek," Marianna says. "It's a thing with him."

A minute later, we walk into Large Marge's Pizza and Sub Shop. Some older kids are sitting at a booth, eating fries, and a man in a suit and tie is reading a newspaper.

A woman behind the counter smiles at us. "What can I get for you, girls?" she asks. I've seen her—Marge—before because my parents love the food here. But usually they do the ordering. Today, I'm in charge.

"I'd like two subs, please," I say.

"Coming right up!" Marge replies, snugging a pair of plastic gloves over her hands. She takes a bread knife and slices open two buns. "What would you like on them?"

I look at the sandwich fixings behind the counter's glass shield and repeat what Mom told me to say this morning. Alphabetically, of course, because librarians are into that. "Cheese, lettuce, peppers, sprouts, tomatoes, and turkey, please."

"Got it," Marge says, going to work on the sandwiches.

"*Two* subs?" Marianna says. "Don't you need three?"

My stomach flip-flops. I glance at Marianna. "Um . . . my dad doesn't like subs," I say. "He'll eat something else later." I turn back to Marge. "Could you put extra peppers on that one?" I point through the glass as she works. "My mom loves them."

"Sure thing," Marge says, adding more peppers to Mom's sub. Red, yellow, green, orange. A pepper rainbow. "Who's your mom?"

"Emily Byrd," I reply. "She's the head librarian at the Oak Hill Public Library."

"Oh, sure!" Marge exclaims. "I know your folks. How're they doing?"

"They're fine," I say. "We're all fine."

Marge nods. "And who might you be?" she asks Marianna, wrapping the sandwiches in paper.

"*I* am Marianna Van Den Heuval," Marianna replies. "I moved here from Seattle this summer. My mom will be coming soon. She's an artist. So is my dad. The only one who doesn't do art in my family is Reuben."

"Your brother?" Marge asks.

Marianna shakes her head. "My stepdad."

"Well, I look forward to meeting your whole family," Marge says.

Marianna nods. "My mom will be here any day now. She promised."

I pay for the subs, then we head out the door.

When we get to the library, I expect Marianna to keep walking straight home. But she heads up the steps with me. "Good-bye?" I say, when I get to the door. "This is the library. You can go home now."

"I know it's the library," Marianna replies. "I'm going in with you."

"*Um*Why?"

"*Um*Hello? Homework? That's what friends do after school, Tweety."

"But won't your stepdad wonder where you are?"

"I texted Reuben from school." She grabs the handle on the door and pulls it open. "Hello, Mrs. Byrd!" she calls out when we get inside. "It's me, Marianna Van Den Heuval! Your daughter is here, safe and sound, just like I promised."

A couple of kids look over from the DVD rack. A woman glances up from her laptop.

Mom appears from behind a bookshelf. "Thank you for letting me know, Marianna. But, please, use your library voice in here."

"This *is* my library voice, Mrs. Byrd," Marianna replies loudly. Then she turns to me. "Don't just stand there, Tweety, start moving chairs. Let's build one of those book hook things you're so crazy about."

"Book *nook*," I correct her, looking at Mom. The library isn't too busy. She gives me a nod.

I set the take-out food on Mom's desk and lead Marianna to a back corner. We crawl under one of the reading tables, cage ourselves in with chairs, and take out the math worksheets Ms. Little gave to us at the end of the day.

"Math is one of my best subjects," Marianna

tells me. "My friends are always asking me to help them solve their problems."

"I can solve my own problems," I say, taking out a pouch of pencils and erasers I keep in my backpack.

"You must make a lot of mistakes," Marianna says, watching as I dump out the pouch. "You've got, what? Five erasers there? I saw even more in your desk at school."

"Collecting erasers is my hobby," I explain. "I've got lots of different kinds. Animals, flowers, rainbows, fruit, candy . . . I've even got one that's a hamburger you can take apart and put back together again."

Marianna sniffs. "*My* hobby is collecting sea glass."

I frown. "What's that?"

Marianna straightens up and shows me her necklace with the milky blue pendant. "It's *glass* that comes from the *sea*," she explains in a teacher voice. "You know, bottles and jars that end up in the ocean? The rocks break them into little pieces. Then the waves tumble them around and around, pounding down their sharp edges so the jagged parts are smooth. When they finally wash up onshore, all that ugly glass has been changed into something pretty, see?" She twirls the pendant. "My mom's house is right by the ocean. We comb the beaches in Seattle for sea glass all the time."

"You're going to need a new hobby, then," I say. "We don't have any oceans in Oak Hill."

"There's a lake in town," Marianna says, adjusting the necklace. "You live by it. As soon as my mother gets here, we'll hunt for glass there."

"You better hurry before the snow falls and the lake freezes."

Marianna cocks her head. "What do you mean . . . *freezes*?"

"Lakes are made from *water*," I explain, like I'm the teacher now. "Water *freezes* when it gets cold. The ice on Pickerel Lake gets so thick you can walk on it. People even drive their cars across it. My dad sets up a little house out there every winter. It has a hole in the floor so he can cut through the ice and stay warm and snug inside while he fishes."

Marianna blinks. "Are you fibbing me, Tweety?"

I shake my head. "It's the truth."

"Weird," Marianna replies. "I wonder why the ocean doesn't freeze like that."

I shrug, then move a chair aside and look around for Mom. I spot her a few tables over. "Mom?" I call out in a loud whisper.

She glances up from a book she's showing to the woman with the laptop. "What is it, Wren?" she whispers back.

"Why don't oceans freeze?"

Mom purses her lips. "Look it up," she says, then starts talking quietly with the woman again.

I crawl back inside the book nook. Marianna and I huddle over my phone while I type in the question.

Why don't oceans freeze?

Marianna reads the answer that pops up. "Some oceans *do* freeze when the temperature is cold enough. But warm currents, depth, and salt in the water keep many oceans from freezing."

I click off my phone. "So that's the answer," I say. "Oceans have currents and salt, plus they're deep. Pickerel Lake is too little. No salt."

Marianna nods. "True, but Pickerel Lake doesn't freeze solid, or the fish would die. So that makes it big too." She shrugs. "Some things are like that, Tweety. Big and little at the same time. Weird."

Stretching out her legs, Marianna starts talking in her teacher voice again. Like she's bigger than me.

"This will be fun!" Mom says later as she pushes aside papers and pencils on her desk to make room for our supper. "We can have an indoor picnic." I set my sub on the corner of Mom's desk and pull up a chair. Marianna left a few minutes ago. Her stepdad sent a text saying supper was almost ready, so she should come home. I wonder what she's eating. Crab and caviar? She said her stepdad likes to cook. I bet he even sets the table for supper.

I unwrap my sub and take a bite.

"How was your day?" Mom asks, unwrapping her sandwich too. She opens two bottles of water she keeps by her desk.

"It was fine," I reply.

"Any homework?"

"I finished it already."

"You and Marianna seem to be getting along," Mom comments. "You're both good readers. Her stepdad stopped by earlier to return her books. Did you know he grew up here? Your dad and he played basketball together in high school."

I hate when she says *your dad* instead of just Dad. Like he belongs to only me now.

"Marianna must be sad about her mother's plans changing," Mom adds, then takes a bite from her sandwich.

I look up from my sub. "What do you mean?"

Mom swallows and takes a sip of water. "Didn't Marianna tell you? Her mother's project has been delayed. Reuben said it will be another month, at least, before she moves here." She bites into her sandwich again.

My eyes scrunch with confusion. "Are you sure

Marianna knows? She was just saying her mom will be moving here any day."

Mom shrugs, chewing. "I assume she knows. Reuben didn't act like it was a secret or—" She makes a strange face, then drops her sub and grabs some water.

"What is it?" I ask. "Don't you like your sandwich?"

"Hot!" she says, waving her hand in front of her mouth. She takes a gulp of water. "Peppers!"

"I asked for extra," I say. "I know how much you like them."

"I like *sweet* peppers," Mom replies, after she catches her breath. "Your dad likes the spicy kind." She wipes a tear from her eye and grabs a tissue to blow her nose.

I slump. "Sorry."

"It's okay," Mom replies, picking bits of peppers from her sandwich. "Next time you'll know."

I sigh, chewing slowly.

Next time doesn't feel like a picnic.

Next time feels like a chore.

When Mom and Dad told me they were getting

a divorce, they said it had nothing to do with me.

But *I'm* the one who has to walk to the library with Marianna Van Den Heuval.

I'm in charge of getting supper now.

I'm eating at a desk, surrounded by stacks of books and messages scribbled on sticky notes, instead of at a table with dishes and silverware.

I'm the one without a best friend.

Mom's phone chirps. She looks at the screen. "Chew fast," she tells me. "It's your dad. I'm not getting it."

I swallow and snatch the phone from Mom before it goes to voicemail.

"Hello? Dad?" I say.

"Hey, Squirt!" he says. "I thought I was calling your mom's phone."

"You are," I say. "I'm here with her, at the library. Did you want to talk to her?"

"Actually, I tried calling your phone a bunch of times, but you weren't picking up."

"Oh!" I say. "Ms. Little makes us turn off the ringers during school. I must have forgotten to turn mine back on. Why are you calling? It's

Thursday. You're not in charge of me until tomorrow."

Dad chuckles. "I can call you any day of the week, Squirt. Got time for some quick questions? It's been a while."

I sit up taller. "Okay! You start."

Dad thinks for a minute. "How was your first day of school?" he asks.

"Good!" I reply.

Mom glances over. Then she looks away again and takes a sip of water.

"What did you do?"

"The usual. Math. Reading. Spelling. I got put in the Red reading group. Ms. Little didn't say so, but I think it's got the best readers in it."

"Way to go, Squirt! Do you still like your new teacher? Or do I have to find a replacement?"

"Yes! I mean, no! I like Ms. Little a lot."

"Does she serve spaghetti and meatballs for milk break?"

"No!"

"Did she call on you during math today?"

"Yes."

"Did you know the answer?"

"On the second try."

"Good job! Are your classmates nice?"

"Mostly."

"Did you kiss any boys?"

"Da-ad!"

"Heh-heh. Do you have any homework?"

"No. Marianna and I just finished."

"Marianna?"

"The new girl."

"So you've made a new friend?"

"Not exactly. She acts like the boss of us."

"I see. At least you haven't made any enemies, right?"

I don't answer, thinking about Amber.

Mom looks at me and taps her watch. *Chop-chop,* she mouths, with no sound.

"Still there, Squirt? That was a joke, by the way."

"I'm still here, but I should finish eating now. Can we talk later?"

"Sure thing," Dad says. "I didn't realize it was suppertime already."

"It's not. I mean, it is. I mean . . . I'm eating at the library because Mom is working."

"Got it," Dad says. "How about I call later to say good night? Turn your phone on, okay? When do you go to bed these days? Six o'clock?" He chuckles again.

I roll my eyes. "Mom says I can stay up until nine this year."

"Call you before then. Now, put your mother on the phone for a minute, please."

I brighten. "You want to talk to Mom?"

"Yes, Squirt, I do."

"Okay, just a minute! Here she is." I hold the phone out to Mom. "Dad wants to talk to you."

Mom sets down her sandwich slowly. She wipes her fingers on a napkin. Then she takes the phone. "What is it?" she asks. *Pause.* "Of course she knows about riding the bus. I made a schedule." *Pause.* "Don't be ridiculous, no one is keeping her from calling you." *Pause.* "She has school now, Jeff. Her schedule is diff—what? That's not my responsibility! You'll have to remind her yourself." *Pause. Pause. Pause.* "Yes, I'm still here, but

I'm at work. Talk to her about it this weekend. I'm hanging up now."

Mom sets down her phone. She refolds the paper over her unfinished sub and throws it in the trash.

"What's wrong?" I ask in my smallest voice. "You sounded mad."

Mom wipes crumbs from her desk. "No one is mad. Your dad was just confused about . . . your schedule. Wren, you know you can call him any day of the week, don't you?"

I didn't really know that, but I nod.

"And you may call me on the weekends, if you wish. Understood?"

I nod again.

"Good," Mom says, brushing the last of the crumbs from her fingers. "That's done. Now, chop-chop. Finish your supper. It'll be time to go home soon."

"I'm finished," I say, pushing my sub away. "May I be excused from the table? I mean, desk?"

"Yes, but you've hardly eaten a thing."

"I'm not hungry," I say, slipping out of my chair and going back to the book nook.

Lying down, I rest my head on my backpack. Then I close my eyes and think back to when I was little. I'm snuggled up in my jammies. Dad is reading me a bedtime story. Mom comes in and tucks the blankets around me. I smile as they both kiss me good night, then walk out of my room, hand in hand.

I open my eyes. *When was the last time they held hands?* I ask myself. But I can't remember the answer.

Unzipping my backpack, I take out my phone and turn on the ringer. I wish I could call Amber. We've always talked to each other about everything, even the bad stuff. But this secret is worse than bad. And now she seems happier talking to Marianna than to me.

I look up the word *happy*.

Happy
• Feeling pleasure because of your life situation
• Delighted
• Pleased
• Content

Next, I type *content*.

Content
- Glad
- Satisfied
- Not needing more

I click off my phone and lie down again. *When did Mom and Dad stop being happy? I ask myself. How come no one told me we needed more?*

CHAPTER 9

Dad was supposed to stop by yesterday and pick up half of my clothes to keep at his cabin, but he got busy at work and couldn't make it.

So now I have to bring enough clothes for the weekend to school. Mom told me to put everything in my sleepover bag, but if I do that, the other girls will think I changed my mind about going to the party. I already told them I'm helping my dad this weekend. I can't change lies now.

I take the clothes Mom laid out for me and stuff them into my backpack. Underwear at the bottom, so no one sees them. Then pajamas, then a pair of jeans and a couple T-shirts. Shakespeare hops up on my bed as I try to squeeze in my schoolbooks too. "Sorry, Shakespeare," I say. "I wish I could sneak you along for the weekend, but it's hard to pack a cat." I pick him up and stroke his soft fur. He purrs so loudly I can feel it inside my chest. "I don't know why I'm the one who has to go away when none of this was my idea."

Shakespeare rubs against my jaw. I kiss the top of his head. "Try not to miss me too much," I whisper. "I'll see you Sunday night." Then I set him down and tug the zipper closed on my backpack, which isn't easy because it's so fat. I lug it onto my back and look at myself in my mirror. "Great," I say with a sigh. "I'm a turtle."

Shakespeare rubs a figure eight around my ankles.

When I get to my classroom, the first person I see is Marianna Van Den Heuval.

She watches as I squish my fat backpack into my cubby and then wiggle my books out carefully, so my clothes stay put. But they bulge out anyway.

"What's that?" Marianna asks, poking her nose over my shoulder to get a better look. "Pajamas? Are you coming to Am's sleepover? I was hoping you would change your mind! We're going to have *So. Much. Fun!* I packed my cutest pajamas and my most *secret* diary. You won't believe the stuff I've written in it!"

"I'm not going to the sleepover," I reply, stuffing down my clothes and zipping my backpack shut. "I just had to bring some extra clothes in case I get dirty while I'm helping my dad." I practiced that lie while I was walking to school this morning.

Marianna makes a face. "Can't you just go home and change if you get dirty? And why would you need pajamas?"

"In case we work late and I get tired," I reply. "We'll be all the way across the lake from my . . . I mean . . . our house. I can't go home to change unless my dad drives me, or I swim."

My lies are lame, but Marianna doesn't seem

interested in my answers this time. She grabs her sleepover bag and starts digging through it. "Can you keep a secret, Tweety?" she asks in a low voice.

"Yes," I reply. "I'm very good at keeping secrets."

Marianna glances around to make sure no one is snooping. Then she pulls something from her backpack that's hidden in her fist. "Hold out your hand and close your eyes and I will give you a *big* surprise!"

I make a face. "What is it? A frog or something?"

Marianna smirks. "Of course not. That would be mean. I only give my friends nice surprises. Now hold out your hand."

My hands stay still.

"You have to *trust* me, Tweety. Hurry, before the other girls get here!"

I do not trust Marianna Van Den Heuval. But I don't want to be standing here with her, in the coatroom, when the other girls arrive. What if Marianna mentions my pajamas to them? They might start asking questions too. I close my eyes and hold out my hand.

Marianna drops something into it. It doesn't feel squishy, like a frog. It feels firm and curved, like a question mark.

I open my eyes and see an orca eraser in the palm of my hand.

"Surprise!" Marianna cries. "It's from Seattle. I knew you'd like it. I'm giving souvenirs to all the girls at the sleepover tonight. Amber is getting a Space Needle charm, Phoebe will have my Mount Rainier magnet, and Eleanor gets a seagull key chain. Since you won't be there, I had to give you the orca eraser early. *Don't* tell the others."

"I won't," I say, unzipping a pocket on my backpack and taking out my pencil pouch. I tuck the orca inside. "Thanks, Marianna," I say. "I don't have an orca in my eraser collection."

Marianna smiles. "Good thing I'm here."

When the other girls arrive, they drop their sleepover bags and rush up to Marianna, bouncing with excitement and babbling about all the fun they'll have tonight. I squish my backpack into my cubby as far as it will go and stand in front of it to block their view, but everyone is too busy talking to notice my backpack.

"You guys will die when I tell you this!" Amber says excitedly. "Ivory is going to do our *nails* and give us *facials*! I think Mom is paying her, but who cares? We'll get to wear mascara and everything!"

Eleanor gasps. "I've never worn mascara before!"

"Me either!" Phoebe adds, pushing up her glasses.

"*I* have," Marianna says importantly. "For my mother's wedding, last spring. *I* was the maid of honor. I wore eye shadow and lipstick too." The girls gape at her, impressed.

"We should plan our weddings tonight!" Amber says. "We can write everything down in our diaries, including which boys we'll *marry*!"

Phoebe and Eleanor squirm like they have to pee. "I brought one of my sister's movies," Phoebe says breathlessly. "It's got kissing in it!"

"That's nothing," Marianna says. "I brought a *surprise* for everyone." She gives me a sideways glance. "Only Tweety knows."

Phoebe and Eleanor rush over to me.

"Tell us the secret, Wren, *pleeease*?" Phoebe tugs on my arm, pleading.

"Pleeeese?" Eleanor tugs on my other arm.

I shake my head. "I promised I wouldn't tell. But I think you'll like it!"

This only makes them tug harder.

Amber gawks at Marianna. "It's *my* party! If anyone should be in on a secret, it's *me*. Why would you tell Wren at all? She's not even coming."

"*That's* why I told her," Marianna replies. "Relax, Am. You'll find out tonight."

Amber crosses her arms. She looks as unrelaxed as a fencepost.

At lunch, Amber scoots in next to Marianna instead of taking the empty seat next to me. At recess, she grabs a ball and saves the four-square court, then calls over Marianna, Phoebe, and Eleanor to play. During milk break, she keeps the last carton of chocolate for herself, sticking me with white. In phys ed, she picked all the other girls for her kickball team, but not me. When it was my turn to kick, she pitched the ball so bouncy I couldn't even get it past the pitcher's mound. She grabbed it and nailed me on the way to first base. She had to have known it hurt, but she didn't say she was sorry, which stung more than getting hit.

After school, the girls pile their sleepover stuff into Amber's van and drive off together, talking and laughing the whole time.

My backpack straps dig into my shoulders like I'm carrying cement blocks instead of my books and weekend clothes. I have to find Bus #5. It should be after #4, but it's not. Walking up and down the sidewalk, I read bus numbers, hoping no one notices and asks me why I'm looking for a bus at all.

When I finally find #5, it's packed with kids—big ones toward the back, little ones up front. Bowtie is sitting in the middle. Actually, both Bo and Ty are up on their knees, bugging some girls from Mr. Ortega's class who are sitting behind them.

Quickly, before they turn around, I plop into

an empty seat across the aisle and start shaking off my fat backpack.

"Hi," someone says.

I look across the seat and see Ruby Olson.

"Oh, hi," I reply. "I didn't see you. Are you saving this seat?"

Ruby shakes her head. "Are you going to a sleepover or something?"

"No," I say, setting my backpack by my feet as the bus pulls away from the school.

"My dad is fixing up a cabin on the other side of Pickerel Lake. I'm helping him this weekend."

"Which cabin?" Ruby asks.

I shrug. "It belongs to somebody named Kermit. He's a man, not a frog."

Ruby snorts a laugh. "Kermit *Olson*? He's my grandpa. I didn't know he was getting his cabin fixed up. Usually he just rents it out to people on summer vacation."

"Maybe he wants to make it look nice before next summer?" I offer, hoping her grandpa hasn't said anything to her about Dad renting the cabin.

Ruby nods like this makes sense. "It needs

some fixing. Sometimes my brothers and I use it to warm up when we're out on the lake in the winter. I think mice use it to warm up too." She snickers.

I gulp and look past her, out the window. Before long, we pass by Mom's house. I try to catch a glimpse of Shakespeare, sitting in my bedroom window, but Ruby is in the way and I don't want her to wonder why it's so important that I see him.

Suddenly, my braid gets a sharp tug.

"Ouch!"

"Are you lost, little bird?"

I whip around to see Bo's goofy grin.

Ty giggles next to him, bouncing on the bus seat. "Yeah, Birdbrain, are you lost?"

"No!" I sneer, rubbing my head. "Leave me alone."

I face forward.

Bo pulls my braid again. "Ding dong! Anybody home?"

"Stop it!" I shout, shoving him away.

"Knock it off, Bo," Ruby says, through gritted teeth. "I'm warning you . . ."

"Oooo . . ." Bo says, fake shivering. "I'm sooo scared!"

"Yeah . . ." Ty says, aping Bo's shivers. "We're sooo scared!"

Bo leans in. "Whatcha gonna do, Rubes? Sic your brothers on us?"

"Nope," Ruby replies. "I can handle you pea brains myself."

Bo waves her off and turns to me again. "If you're not lost, Byrd, how come you're on my bus?"

"None of your business," I grumble.

"*Everything* is my business," Bo says, stroking his invisible beard.

"Yeah, *everything* is our business!" Ty puts in. He starts reaching for my braid.

Ruby flies to her knees and pounces at Ty, grabbing him by the scruff of his skinny neck.

"Owwwiiieee, Rubeeeey!" he wails.

Ruby digs her fingernails in deeper. "Are you gonna leave us alone?"

"Yes, yes, I swear!" Ty howls, squirming under Ruby's grip.

She lets go.

Ty falls back, rubbing his neck.

"Sheesh, Rubes," Bo says, leaning in again. "We were just joking around."

The bus slows to a stop and Bo and Ty scramble down the aisle and out the door. They look up at our window as the bus pulls out again, scratching their armpits like monkeys and sticking their tongues out at Ruby and me.

We make monkey faces back at them.

"Do you think they will ever mature?" I ask Ruby as the bus heads down the road again.

"Doubt it," she replies. "I should know. I've got three brothers." She fiddles with the zipper on her hoodie, glancing at me like there's something else she wants to say. "If you get bored with helping your dad this weekend . . . you can always . . . if you want . . . hike down to my house. It's not far from Grandpa Kermit's cabin."

"Oh," I say. "Um, thanks, but I think I'm going to be really busy. Helping my dad."

"Sure," Ruby says as the bus stops again and more kids pile off. "I'm just saying, you know, if you get bored."

We ride along without talking until the bus stops again.

"C'mon, Roo." A big boy with shaggy hair that's as red as Ruby's looks back at her as he heads down the aisle. "This is our stop."

"Gotta go," Ruby says, getting up and scooting past me. "See ya, Wren."

"Yeah," I say. "See ya."

Ruby's brother knuckle-rubs her head as they walk up a long dirt driveway that leads to a little white house and a big red barn.

Ruby ducks out from under him and gives me a wave.

I wave too, but we're already heading down the road again.

CHAPTER 10

★

Are Toadstools Poisonous?

Dad is sitting on the steps of his run-down cabin, drinking a cup of coffee, as the bus pulls to a stop at the end of the dirt driveway. I'm relieved Bo and Ty already got off the bus. They won't wonder why I'm being dropped off at this shack.

Dad is still wearing a dusty T-shirt, jeans, and his heavy work boots. His truck and tool trailer are parked in the driveway.

He sets down his coffee and gets to his feet as I walk up the drive. "Hey, Squirt!" he says, giving me a hug. "Are you ready for a grand tour? Thought we'd start with the lake. It's the cabin's best feature."

"Okay," I say.

"You want to ask any questions, or should I?" Dad asks.

"You," I reply.

Dad sets my backpack next to his coffee cup and steers me into the side yard as we shuffle through the fallen leaves that are scattered across the matted grass. The lawn could use a haircut.

"You look a little down, Squirt. How did the bus ride go?" Dad asks, beginning the game.

"It was fine," I reply.

"Any trouble?"

"No. Just boys. I can deal with them."

"That's my girl. How was school?"

"The same as usual."

"Did you have a spelling quiz today?"

"Yes. I aced it."

"Boom! Did you take a trip to Mars?"

Giggle. "No."

"Would you *like* to take a trip to Mars?"

"Yes! With you?"

"Sure. How about a week from Tuesday?"

I giggle some more.

"How's Shakespeare these days?" Dad continues.

"Good. He misses you."

"I have to admit, I miss that fur ball too. Do you have any homework?"

"Some. Not a lot."

"Do you have any fleas?"

"Da-ad."

"Can you say the alphabet backwards?"

"Z . . . Y . . . X . . . um . . . W . . . um . . . no."

"Do you like having your own phone?"

"Yes!"

"And you know you can call me, right?"

"Yes."

"Even for no big reason, okay?"

"Okay."

Dad puts his big, warm hand on my shoulder. "Here's the lake."

Waves chop against the lake's rocky shoreline. A breeze blows against my face now that we're clear of the trees. Clumps of soggy leaves blanket the rocks as the water thumps against them. A big tree lies across the shore, its trunk thick and rough like an elephant's leg. I can see a snag of fishing line caught in its dead branches. Kids must fish from that tree in the summer. I've seen this lake lots of times before, but always from the other side. It's still the same lake, but it looks different from over here.

"Look," Dad says, pointing. "Straight across from here is the park. We can hop on the bike path, just down the road, and pedal all the way around the lake. If you squint, you can see the top of the big playground slide." Dad gives me a sideways glance. "The slide looks little from here, doesn't it, Squirt? Not nearly as scary, this far away."

Dad and Mom were with me the day I shot down that slide in my slippery swimsuit and got spit onto the hard dirt. I was just a little kid then, so it scared me to tears. Mom stood me up and brushed me off. She told me I was fine, then pushed a juice box into my hands. But I couldn't stop crying. Not even when other kids wandered over, watching me. Finally, Dad stepped in and scooped me up like we were roughhousing. He carried me away, whispering funny questions in my ear, until I finally stopped sobbing and started laughing again. Then we sat quietly on a bench, and looked at the lake, while I drank my juice box and Mom repacked the picnic basket.

"I see it," I say. "You're right, the slide looks little now." Then I look past the park and catch a glimpse of Mom's house through the trees. I wonder if she's home yet, or if she's still at work. Will she remember to feed Shakespeare? That's always my job. Will she make popcorn and watch a movie tonight? And read another chapter from *Charlotte's Web,* even if I'm not there to listen?

"Watch your step," Dad says as we walk back toward the cabin. A lumpy mound of brown yuckiness is poking up through the damp leaves.

"Ew . . ." I say, crouching down for a closer look at the weird blob. If Amber were here, we'd make believe it was alien brains. "What *is* that?"

"Toadstools," Dad says, leaning in.

"Are toadstools poisonous?" I ask, poking the blob with a stick.

Dad shrugs. "You never know where a toad's butt has been."

I smirk at Dad's toad joke. "*Butt*-er not touch them." He laughs and takes my hand as I step around the toadstools and follow him to the cabin's back steps. Dad props open the storm door with his foot so he can unlock the cabin's back door. I reach out to hold the storm door for him, but my hand goes right through it because there's no glass in the bottom panel. My knuckles punch Dad's leg.

"Oof," he says. "Nice left hook, Squirt."

I rub my knuckles. "Knock, knock," I say.

"Who's there?" Dad replies.

"Better fix," I say.

"Better fix who?"

"Better fix the broken door."

Dad chuckles, then ruffles my hair. He opens the cabin door and steps inside. "Welcome home, Wren."

Sitting on the bottom bunk in my new bedroom, I bounce a little. The bed squeaks, but not in a creepy way. Amber would probably say it sounds like mouse giggles. The top bunk doesn't have any bedding on it. The walls are the same color as the toadstools in the yard.

The whole cabin is tiny—I can see most of it from my bedroom. Just a teeny kitchen with a round table and three mismatched chairs. The living room has a small couch, Dad's recliner, and a TV sitting on top of his desk. The picture of Dad and me on the logjam ride hangs above it. Around the corner, there's a short hallway leading to the bathroom and Dad's bedroom.

"Sorry about the color," Dad says, watching my eyes from the doorway. "I can ask Kermit if he will let us repaint in here." He looks around my little room. The bunk bed, a tiny desk, and a dresser for my clothes take up most of the space.

"Can we paint it orange?" I ask.

Dad looks at me with surprise. "Orange? I thought your favorite color was blue."

"It used to be, but I switched to orange this summer." It might seem strange to choose a new favorite color when everything else around me was changing. But picking a new favorite color was the only choice that belonged to me.

"I got you some pencils and notebooks," Dad says, stepping over to the desk. "Sorry, they're not orange." He picks up one of the notebooks. It's small, like the one Ms. Little gave to Marianna. The cover is light blue. "I thought we could hang a shelf for your knickknacks, get some posters for the walls . . ." He scuffs his boot across the dark floorboards. "A rug or two . . ."

Dad sighs, his shoulders sagging. He takes off his baseball cap and rubs the back of his neck before sitting next to me. "You deserve better than this, Wren," he says in a low voice, even though no one else is here to listen. "A lot better. But this is the best I can do for now."

Usually, Dad's eyes are bright with a smile or sparkle with mischief, but tonight they look gray and tired, which makes me feel halfway between sad and scared.

"I've always wanted a bunk bed," I say, trying to sound cheerful.

Dad's eyebrows go up. "You have?"

I nod and tap the bunk above me. "I can pretend I'm a pirate in a crow's nest, or a princess in a turret."

The corners of Dad's eyes crinkle a little. "Princess Wren," he says, putting his hat on my head. It comes down over my eyes. "There, now you've got a crown."

I smile.

Dad's phone rings. He steps out to take the call while I hang his hat on my desk chair and pull my phone from my hoodie pocket. I click up the screen and tap out a word.

Toadstool
- A fungus, similar to a mushroom
- Often poisonous

"I was right, toadstools are poisonous," I say to Shakespeare, before I remember he's not here.

Tucking away my phone, I unzip my backpack and put my homework on my desk. Then I tuck my weekend clothes in the dresser. I toss the little blue notebook and a package of pens onto the top bunk and climb the ladder at the end of the bed.

Sitting on the bare mattress, I start drawing swirls and curlicues on the notebook cover. I'm not as good at drawing as Marianna, but I do okay.

She said she has lots of diaries, but I've never kept one before. I take out my phone again.

Diary
- A record of daily events
- A book used for personal reflection

Then I look up *reflection*.

Reflection
- The return of sound or light from a surface
- A turning or bending back
- Serious thinking
- Contemplation

I contemplate for a minute. Then I open my diary to the first page.

Dear Diary,

I'm writing this at Dad's cabin because it's Friday, so this is where I have to be. I hate that we can't all live at our house. Or that Mom and Shakespeare can't live here. Mom wouldn't like the cabin, though. It smells like our basement after it rains. And the curtains on the windows don't match the furniture. Dad doesn't care about that stuff, but I don't think he likes living here either. I wonder who started this whole divorce thing. Was it Mom? Was it Dad? Or did they pinkie-swear at the exact same time? Mom is stressed. Dad looks tired. Why would they do something if it doesn't make us happy?

Amber is having a sleepover tonight. All the girls are there, except me. I wonder if they're baking brownies like Amber and I always do. I mean, did. We'd turn on a movie, crawl under a blanket, and eat the whole pan while the brownies were still gooey and warm. Most times, we wouldn't even watch the movie because we were too busy talking, and laughing, and telling secrets.

"Hungry, Squirt?" Dad pokes in from the living room.

"A little," I say, closing my diary. "Was that Mom on the phone?"

Dad shakes his head. "New client. I just got hired for a big remodel. Should keep me busy for months."

"That's good, right?" I say, even though I'm disappointed it wasn't Mom calling.

Dad nods. "Very good!" He smiles. "How about we celebrate with a Large Marge Pizza Supreme? I'll place the order while you pick out a movie. What do you say? Couch picnic?"

"Okay," I say. "Couch picnic. Movies and a pizza. Extra cheese, please. No mushrooms."

Dad winks and ducks out of my room. A moment later I hear him talking on his phone. "Hey, Marge, it's Jeff Byrd. Good! How are you? That's nice to hear. Say, can you fix up a Supreme for Wren and me? Thanks. Extra cheese, please. Hold the toadstools."

CHAPTER 11

★

Is Not Telling the Same as Lying?

Dad makes chocolate chip pancakes and bacon for breakfast the next morning. "To celebrate your first week of school," he says, turning on the TV so I can watch Saturday cartoons while I eat. But I'm so happy he remembered the pancakes and bacon, I don't care about the cartoons. I open a bottle of syrup and pour it over the pancakes, then take a big bite. It tastes like home. I can practically feel Shakespeare rubbing against my legs, and smell Mom's perfume.

"I thought we'd run into town this morning," Dad says, sitting down next to me with a plate of food and a cup of coffee. "I need to pick up a few things at the hardware store. Then we could drive out to the mall and get some new stuff for your room."

"I don't need any new things," I say, nibbling a slice of bacon.

"Sure you do," Dad replies. "We'll be living here at least through the winter. Maybe next spring we can look for a better place, but for now we need to turn this shack into a home."

"But why can't we just live at *our* house?"

"This *is* our house now, Squirt. Yours and mine."

"But . . . Mom told me you're not divorced yet, only separated. What if you change your mind? Mom doesn't seem happy. I think she misses you . . . What if she wants you to come home?"

"Wren . . ."

"It's true! You can still change your mind. Then everything would be fixed. We could be a family again. It's not too late."

I sit back in my chair, breathing hard and watching the syrup sink into my pancakes. Dad sits quietly, staring at his food too. A cartoon bear sings goofy songs on the TV.

"We're still a family, Wren," Dad finally says, in a low voice. "Divorce can't change that." He reaches over to squeeze my hand, but I pull it away.

"You're wrong." I stand up so fast my chair tips over. "A divorce changes everything."

I run into my bedroom and slam the door. Then I climb up to my top bunk, fall down onto the bare mattress, and cry, with no pillow to bury my face in, and no blanket to clutch, and no cat to cuddle.

If I were home, Mom would come in and pat my back and tell me that's enough crying now, because everything is fine.

But Mom's not here, and Dad doesn't come in.

When my crying finally settles to an ache in my throat, I hear Dad moving around in the kitchen, picking up my chair, carrying breakfast dishes to the sink, scraping pancakes and bacon into the trash. Then the TV clicks off.

There's a knock on my door a minute later. I sit up.

"What do you say then, Squirt?" Dad asks, looking in. "Shall we run into town? Stop out at the mall and pick up a few things?"

I rub the tears from my cheeks. What else can I do? I nod.

When we get to the mall later, we're both hungry from not finishing breakfast, so we go to the food court first thing. It's super-busy with lots of people eating lunch. Kids are running around, babies are crying, grown-ups are laughing and trying to talk over all the other voices. Dad takes my hand and we "excuse me" through the lines of people waiting to order food. It feels weird to be here with Dad. Usually, he and I only come to the mall to see a movie or to buy Mom a Christmas present. Who will help me buy a present for her this year? Is Dad allowed to? I wonder if Marianna would know.

"What are you hungry for, Squirt?" Dad asks, looking up and down the row of food counters. "Burgers? Pizza? Tacos? Egg rolls?"

"Mom always gets the veggie stir-fry on brown

rice," I reply. "She says it's the only healthy option."

"I suppose that's true," Dad says, rubbing his neck and taking another look around. "Too bad the *un*healthy stuff tastes so good. Tell you what, how about we get tacos and throw a little lettuce and tomato on them? That'd make 'em healthy."

Dad gives me a hopeful look.

"I suppose that would be okay," I reply.

Dad grins. "I'll get in line. You grab that table over there, before it's gone."

I look where Dad is pointing and see one empty table in the middle of a sea of people. I hurry over and sit down.

Dad gives me a thumbs-up, then gets in line for tacos.

"Look, Mommy, it's Wren!" I hear someone shout behind me. "Hi, Wren! Hi!"

I turn around and see Slate waving excitedly from a few tables over. Mrs. Lane looks up, sees me, and smiles. Then everyone turns and looks at me—Amber, Marianna, Phoebe, and Eleanor. My stomach sinks to my sneakers. *What are they doing here?*

Mrs. Lane waves me in. "Join us, Wren!" She scoots Slate onto her lap and pats the chair next to her. "Where's your family?"

"My dad is getting food," I call back. "I'm saving a table."

"We're nearly done," she replies. "You can have our spot!" She pats the chair again.

Reluctantly, I walk over to where they're sitting. Phoebe and Eleanor give me friendly smiles. Marianna waves. Amber glances away.

Eleanor offers some fries to me. "We're going to the matinee!"

"That's nice," I say, not taking any fries.

"You should come with us, Tweety," Marianna says.

"She *can't*," Amber cuts in. "Remember? She's *supposed* to be helping her dad this weekend."

"I *am* helping him," I say. "We're just here on our . . . lunch break."

"What's your dad working on these days?" Mrs. Lane asks, wiping ketchup off Slate's chin. He loves ketchup as much as Amber and I do.

"Um . . . he's fixing up an old cabin," I say. "I

mean, *we* are. It needs a new door and paint and stuff."

"Well, that's wonderful," Mrs. Lane replies. "But couldn't he give you the afternoon off? Then you could stay for the movie!"

"But it starts in *Twenty. Minutes. Mom,*" Amber says. "We still have to buy our *tickets*? And get *popcorn*? Wren hasn't even eaten lunch yet."

Mrs. Lane gives Amber a sharp look, but before she can say anything Dad appears with a tray full of food. "Hello, ladies . . ." he says to Mrs. Lane and the girls. ". . . and gentleman," he adds, nodding to Slate. "Good to see you all again."

"Good to see you too, Jeff!" Mrs. Lane replies. She glances past Dad. "Is Emily here? I've been trying to get in touch with her for days."

Dad shakes his head. "It's just Wren and me," he replies. Then he looks at the girls again. "What are you ladies shopping for today?"

"We're not shopping," Amber says. "I had a sleepover last night. Now we're going to a movie. Wren can't come because she's too busy helping you."

I freeze.

Mrs. Lane turns back to Dad. "Wren is *welcome* to join us if you can spare her for the afternoon. We hear she's helping you with a project."

Dad gives me a puzzled look.

I think fast. "I told them about fixing up the cabin."

Dad's face relaxes. "Ah. That."

"Is it one of those fancy summer homes by the lake, Jeff?" Mrs. Lane asks Dad. "I'm always drooling over them when I drive past."

Dad laughs. "*My* cabin? No, it's more of a hunting shack than a summer home."

"Oh! I didn't realize you owned it. Well, I'm sure with Wren's help, you and Emily will have it fixed up in no time! But, really, couldn't you get along without Wren for *one* afternoon? We'd love it if she could—"

"*Mo-om,*" Amber nags. "Can we Go. Now? We're going to miss the *Pre. Views!*"

I tug on Dad's arm. "Let's eat, okay? I don't feel like seeing a movie. And I'm starving." I pull him toward the table I was saving. Thankfully, it's still open.

"Er . . ." Dad says, looking from me to Mrs. Lane. "Looks like she'll have to take a rain check on the movie. Have fun, though!"

"Bye, Wren!" Phoebe and Eleanor call as they carry their food trays to a trash can.

"See you at school, Tweety," Marianna adds before Amber pulls her toward the theater entrance.

"Bye, Jeff," Mrs. Lane calls as she grabs Slate's hand before he runs off. "Say hi to Emily for me, will you?"

Dad nods. "Will do. First chance I get."

Slate slips away. Mrs. Lane chases after him.

We sit down and start unwrapping tacos.

"What was that all about?" Dad asks, pushing a straw into his soda.

I keep unwrapping.

Dad takes a sip from his cup. "Amber had a sleepover and you didn't go? You're going to have to tell me when there's stuff going on, Wren. Your mom used to take care of that sort of thing. It's up to you now, to keep me in the loop."

"I just didn't feel like going, okay?" I pick up

my taco and take a bite, even though I've lost my appetite again.

"Okay," Dad says. "But next time, let me know."

Dear Diary,

Today Dad and I bought some new stuff for the cabin. I got matching pillows and blankets for both bunks, so I can sleep up or down, whichever I want. And some posters to hide the ugly walls in here. I also got a fuzzy orange rug for the floor, and an alarm clock that looks like a cat! Dad bought some pot holders for the kitchen and a boyish rug for the living room. He bought a shelf too, and hung it above my desk, where I'm sitting right now. The shelf is still empty because all of my important things are at Mom's house.

I pause and think about seeing the girls at the mall today. I wonder which movie they saw. And if Ivory gave them makeovers and if they really did plan their weddings. I wonder if Amber will invite me to the next sleepover, or if she's done being friends with me.

Is not telling people something the same as lying? If it is, I think Mom is lying about the divorce. Dad too.

Do they wish it would disappear?

I do.

Unzipping my backpack, I take out my pencil pouch. I want to use some of my glitter gel pens to add more decorations to the cover of my new diary. The pens Dad bought for me don't sparkle.

But when I dig through my pencil pouch, the first thing I pull out is the orca eraser Marianna gave to me yesterday. I forgot all about it. "Do you think the other girls liked their souvenirs?" I ask the eraser. It doesn't answer because erasers can't talk. But Shakespeare isn't here, so I keep asking it questions anyway.

"Do you miss Seattle?"

"Does Marianna?"

"Has she always been so bossy?"

"Does she really have five best friends?"

"Don't tell her I said this, but I think she might be lying. Most bossy girls don't have that many friends."

The orca keeps quiet.

I reach up and set it on my little empty shelf.

CHAPTER 12

★

Why Is Dad Here?

When I get to my classroom on Monday morning, everyone is huddled around the blue bulletin board, looking at the *All About Me!* posters Ms. Little hung there. Marianna's poster is right in the middle of the board. In the *My Best Friend!* space, she drew a picture of a girl with hair as red as Ruby's, only it's as long as mine. Under her smiling face is the name Sasha, Marianna's Seattle friend. There's plenty of room for more faces, but she only drew one. My poster is next to Amber's. I glance at her to see if she noticed I drew her picture for *My Best Friend!* and Marianna didn't.

But she and Marianna are busy laughing at Mitchell. He's pretending to be a news reporter as he reads headlines from different posters. "News flash! Jordan Bacon's favorite food is . . . bacon! Ruby Olson's favorite pet is a man-eating goldfish named Bubbles! And this just in . . . contrary to popular belief, Zach Williams's best friend is not Batman . . . it's me!"

Zach and Mitchell do a high five.

"Cool cat, Byrd," Bo says, pointing at my drawing of Shakespeare. "It looks like an alien."

"Um . . . thanks?" I say because I think he meant it as a compliment.

Bo nods. "Hey, how come you weren't on the bus this morning?"

"Oh . . . um . . . that," I say, looking around to see if anyone is listening in. "I only ride it on Fridays."

"She was helping her dad on a new project," Ruby says.

I nod. I've told the lie so many times now, it even sounds true to me when someone else says it.

"She could have gone to a sleepover." Amber looks at me. "But she didn't want to come."

"Yes, I did," I tell Amber. "But I couldn't."

"She'll come to the next one," Marianna says. "As soon as my mom gets here, I'm going to throw a big bash. I'll even invite you, Ruby Red Punch."

Ruby narrows her eyes. "Sorry, I'm going to be busy," she replies, and walks away.

While Ms. Little meets with one of our reading groups, the rest of us have free time to do extra-credit worksheets, or play quiet games together, or go on the classroom computer. Amber is in the first reading group. So are Phoebe and Eleanor, so I take a book from our classroom library and sit down on a carpet square in the corner to read. A moment later, Marianna is standing over me.

"Hello, Tweety," she says, dumping a jigsaw puzzle on the floor between us. "I'll let you make a puzzle with me."

Marianna sits down and starts flipping over puzzle pieces. I set aside my book and help her.

"How was the movie on Saturday?" I ask.

Marianna shrugs. "I'm not sure. I fell asleep halfway through it."

"Why? Did you guys stay awake all night at Amber's party?"

"Well, Eleanor sure didn't. She snores like a grizzly bear!"

I snicker. "That's true. I've been at sleepovers with her before."

Marianna glances over her shoulder at Amber. She's reading aloud to her group, so Marianna turns back to me and leans in. "Don't tell Am I said this," she whispers, "but, truth? Her party was mostly b-o-r-i-n-g. Do you know what that spells, Tweety?"

"Yes, Marianna," I say. "I can spell."

"Boring," she tells me anyway. "I forgot to pack my phone, so I couldn't text any of my friends. Then Amber decided we should read our diaries to each other."

"Did Amber read hers? What did she write?"

" 'Blah, blah, blah . . . I ate eggs for breakfast. Blah, blah, blah . . . I'm so mad at Wren . . . Blah, blah, blah . . . I watched a show on TV.' " Marianna lets her head loll to the side, like she's fallen asleep, then straightens up again. "See what I mean? Boring. She didn't even have a juicy

142
★ ★ ★

reason for why you two are fighting. Why are you, anyway? All she said was you left for the summer without saying good-bye."

"I'm not fighting, she is," I reply. "I couldn't help not saying good-bye. No one told me I had to . . . that we were . . . leaving so fast."

"It doesn't matter, Tweety, because as soon as she started writing about being friends with me, she stopped writing about you. But then Phoebe and Elea*snore* wanted to read from their diaries. *Yawn.* They *begged* me to read mine too, of course, but after listening to theirs, I told a little fib and said I forgot to bring mine. I don't share my secrets with just anybody."

Marianna goes back to making the puzzle, but she keeps talking.

"So, how long have you lived in Oak Hill?"

"Since forever," I reply.

"Thought so. I saw a picture of your pet cat on your poster. What's her name?"

"*His* name is Shakespeare."

"Shakespeare? If I had a cat, I'd give him a *cute* name like Cupcake or Muffin."

"I didn't get to name him," I say. "My mom did."

"Huh. What about your dad? Were you fibbing when you said he lives in an igloo on the lake all winter?"

I rattle my head, confused. Then I realize what she's talking about. "He doesn't live in an igloo. It's a tiny house, just for ice fishing."

"How tiny?"

"Tinier than any house you've ever lived in."

Marianna sniffs. "Doubt it," she mumbles.

"What do you mean?"

"Nothing. How many erasers do you have in your collection?"

"Forty-nine. No, wait. Fifty, counting the orca."

Marianna smiles. "Aren't you ever going to invite me over so I can see your whole collection?"

Silence.

"I've been to Am's house lots of times. Don't tell her I said this, but her family isn't like yours and mine."

I freeze as I pick up a puzzle piece. "W-what do you mean? My family isn't like yours."

Marianna's face goes blank. "You didn't draw

any brothers or sisters on your poster. I figured you don't have any either."

"Oh. That. Right."

"Why? What did you think I meant?"

"Nothing."

Marianna shifts her legs and hunts for puzzle pieces again. "Amber's house is like a circus clown car, you know? All those noisy people crammed into a tiny space. They even act like it's fun! When I was little, I wished for brothers and sisters. Not anymore."

There's a knock on our classroom door. I look up and can't believe my eyes. It's Dad!

I jump up and hurry over to him. "Dad?" I say. "Why are you here? Is something wrong?"

"Hey, Squirt! Everything's fine." He gives me a quick hug, then looks across the room at my teacher. "Sorry to interrupt, Ms. Little, but Wren left her jacket in my truck over the weekend and I thought she might need it. The temp is supposed to drop tonight."

Ms. Little gets up from the reading table, smiling as she walks over to us. "It's not a problem at all," she tells Dad. "I'm always happy to have parents stop by. It's almost time for our milk break. Would you like to join us? We have graham crackers." She smiles again.

Dad chuckles. "That's a hard invitation to pass up, but I've gotta run for now. My schedule is flexible, though, so let me know if you're ever looking for a class chaperone."

Ms. Little brightens even more. "Thank you, Mr. Byrd! Your wife volunteered too. I'll give you both a call."

"You probably have Emily's number. Let me give you mine too."

"I'll give it to her," I say quickly, glancing past Ms. Little. My whole class is looking at us. Marianna is looking right at *me*.

I grab my jacket and start nudging Dad back toward the door. "You should go now," I say. "We're busy. This isn't a good time."

"Okay, okay," Dad says, chuckling again. "I can tell when I'm not wanted. I'll call you tonight, okay?"

I give Dad one last nudge without answering

his question. Then I hurry to my cubby and hang up my jacket.

I stay there for a minute after Dad leaves, making up reasons for why he had to bring the jacket to me in the first place.

When I get back into the classroom, everyone is getting ready for our milk break. I help Marianna pick up the puzzle.

"It's warm today," Marianna says. "Why would you need your jacket? And why did he say he'd call you tonight?"

"He's working out of town this week," I say. "I won't get to see him again until Friday."

Marianna nods like this makes sense, but she's squinting like she has more questions. I put the lid on the puzzle box and quickly carry it away before she can ask them.

CHAPTER 13

Does Dad Ever Cry?

All week long, we do the usual stuff at school. Reading. Spelling. Math. Science. No one asks me any questions I have to answer with a lie. When Marianna and I walk to the library, we only discuss normal things, like how many wrong we got on our math quiz (Me: one. Marianna: two), and which instrument in music is the most babyish (Me: wood blocks. Marianna: the triangle), and which boys are the weirdest (Me: Bowtie. Marianna: Bowtie).

Amber is still acting like Marianna is a new toy that she doesn't want to share with anyone. So

Phoebe and Eleanor play with me at recess while Amber pulls Marianna away to teeter-totter, or to play tetherball, or to jump rope. Phoebe and Eleanor don't ask as many big questions as Marianna, so it's easy to play with them.

Most nights, Dad calls me when I'm getting ready for bed. If Mom is there, she drops whatever she's doing and leaves the room. When I go looking for her later, she's usually sitting with a book on her lap. But she's almost never reading it. And sometimes her eyes look like she's been crying.

Sometimes Dad asks me questions and he reads a chapter from one of the books I left at his house. He always says, "Good night, Squirt. See you Friday." Then I hang up and think about him sitting alone in his little cabin, and wonder if he has an unread book on his lap too. Does Dad ever cry? Does he wish he could come back home?

Now it's Thursday afternoon, and I'm walking to the library with Marianna. "This is so awkward," she says, "but I must be Ms. Little's favorite student! Did you notice she made me line leader twice this week? Everyone else only got to be line leader once."

"I don't keep track of who gets to be line leader," I say, even though I do.

Marianna takes a tube of lip gloss from her pocket. She rubs the gloss on her lips, then holds it out to me. "Have some, Tweety. It's pink lemonade! Am gave it to me the other day. I think she swiped it from her sister."

My belly button tightens a little when she says that because Amber used to give me lip gloss and stuff for no special reason. I take the gloss and smooth some on my lips. Then we stop to look at our reflections in Large Marge's big storefront window.

"My mom won't let me buy tinted lip gloss yet," I say, looking at my pink lips. "I'm only allowed to wear clear."

Marianna looks at me from the corners of her eyes. "Awkward question, but, doesn't your mother let you decide anything for yourself? She didn't even let you name your cat."

"That's because Shakespeare belonged to her

first. See, my dad gave him to my mom for her birthday, when she was pregnant with me. She told him to take the kitten back to the shelter because it was 'completely impractical' to get a pet with a baby on the way.

"But my dad set the kitten on her tummy, which was as big as a basketball because I was inside her, and said, 'Happy impractical birthday.' The kitten curled up and started purring. Mom couldn't stop herself from falling in love with him, so she said, 'Fine, we can keep the kitten. His name is Shakespeare. Now call the hospital because I just had a contraction.'"

"Contraction?" Marianna asks.

"It's like a big stomach cramp," I reply. "I looked it up in the dictionary once. Anyway, I was born that night. So my mom got two birthday presents that year—a new kitten and a new baby . . . me."

"And they lived happily ever after," Marianna says, admiring her reflection in the window.

"That was the best day of my life so far," I say, starting down the sidewalk again.

Marianna barks a laugh. "How can it be your *best* day, Tweety? You can't even remember it."

"So? I got born. I got my cat. *And* I got my favorite story. My parents tell it every year on my birthday."

"My parents used to tell me stories like that too," Marianna says.

I glance at her. "Don't they tell you stories anymore?"

"Of course they do. But now my mom tells them to me. Or my dad does. They don't tell them together." She gives me a shrug. "The stories are the same, they just sound different now."

I give Marianna a sideways glance. Then I dare myself to ask her a question. "*Um*Awkward question, but did it make you mad when your parents, you know, when they . . . got one?"

"Got what?" Marianna asks. "A divorce?"

I nod.

"No," she says. "Not really."

I stop and look at her. "It didn't? I mean . . . if my parents were . . . getting a divorce, I think I would be really mad."

Marianna doesn't answer right away. Then she says, "I was sad. But, also, it was kind of a relief. They loved me and all that, but it was obvi they didn't love each other. They argued all the time. After they split up, things got better."

"How?" I ask. "How did it get better?"

Marianna shrugs. "I don't know, exactly. It just happened, little by little. Why do you want to know?"

I start walking again. "No reason."

By the time we get to the library, my lips are buzzing with more questions.

- Did you hope they'd get back together?
- Do you miss seeing your dad every day?
- Did you ever try to keep it all a secret?
- Wouldn't you rather be a family again?

I'm thinking so hard I walk right past the library.

"*Um*Hello? Earth to Tweety? We're here." Marianna walks up the steps and holds the door open for me.

"It's us, Mrs. Byrd!" she calls out when we get inside. "Did my book about sea glass come in yet?"

Mom looks up from her desk. I think she's given up trying to get Marianna to use a quieter voice in here. "Not yet, Marianna," she replies. "You can be sure I will let you know the moment it does." She looks at me. At my pink lemonade lips, but she doesn't say anything about them. "How was your day, Wren?"

"It was fine," I reply. "Can we build a book nook?"

"*May* we," Mom says, correcting me. "Yes, you may."

As soon as Marianna and I get settled under a table, we empty our school stuff on the floor. The lavender notebook Ms. Little gave to Marianna on the first day of school falls out of her tote bag. It's covered with Marianna's drawings now.

"Did you finish writing your autobiography yet?" I ask, pointing to the notebook.

Marianna picks it up. "Oh, that? I finished it in, like, a day. I'm a really good writer. Now I've just been using it to keep track of questions I have for my mom. When she calls, I check them off my list."

"What kind of questions?" I ask.

Marianna opens her notebook and flips through pages of crossed-off questions until she gets to a page of new ones. "Question number one," she reads. "Where will Dad stay when he comes to visit me?" She looks up, like she wants my opinion.

"Your house is big. Can't he stay with you?"

"My house is *huge,*" Marianna says. "But divorced people can't stay together."

I think for a moment. "There's the Starlight Motel. It's on the lake, just past my mom's . . . um . . . just past our house."

Marianna nods, then picks up a pencil and writes *Star Light Motel* under her first question.

"*Starlight* is one word," I say, watching her write.

"I knew that," Marianna mumbles, erasing the word and rewriting it.

"Question number two . . ." she continues, reading from her notebook. "Why did Tweety lie about her dad going out of town this week?" She blinks at me.

My eyes go wide. I look at her notebook. "That's not written there!"

"So?" Marianna says, closing the cover. "Answer my question."

My mouth goes dry. "I . . . I didn't lie," I stammer.

Marianna makes a face. "Then how come your dad was at my house last night? He's going to fix a bunch of stuff for Reuben."

My heart is hammering against my chest now. "My . . . my dad's working for your stepdad?"

Marianna nods. "He stopped by the other day too. Why did you say he's gone?"

"He's not *gone* gone . . . he's just gone some of the time, and then . . . he comes back and goes again." Quickly, I open my math workbook and turn to our homework page. "What answer did you get for number four?" I ask, like the other conversation is over.

Marianna is still studying me, her eyes as cool as ice. "I don't believe you," she says.

I look at my workbook again. "I think the answer is eight."

Suddenly, Marianna's phone starts ringing,

only it sounds like crashing ocean waves. She scrambles to answer it.

"Mom!" she says excitedly. "Hi . . . ! I miss you too! Yes. No. Just hanging out at the library with that girl I told you about. Wren."

Mom walks over to our book nook and bends down to look inside. "Marianna," she says in a hushed voice. "You'll have to take your phone conversation outside."

Marianna rolls her eyes at Mom, but she crawls out from under the table, still talking loud, and hurries out the big glass doors.

I slowly let out a breath, relieved. By the time she gets back, she will have forgotten all about me lying earlier. Dad's new client must be Marianna's stepdad. Mom said they knew each other in high school. Were they best friends back then? Has Dad told him what's going on?

Marianna's notebook is still lying on the floor. I wonder what other questions she wrote in there.

Marianna is still standing on the steps outside, talking on her phone. I pick up her notebook and look inside.

Questions for Mom:

- *Where will Dad stay when he comes to visit me? Answer: Starlight Motel.*
- *Why does Reuben get to tell me what to do? He's not my dad.*
- *How come it's taking you so long to get here? You promised it wouldn't.*
- *Why can't we live in the big house and let the guests stay in the cottage? That makes Way. More. Sense.*
- *Did you get the bracelet I sent for Sasha? I can't find her address. I've texted her a million times since we got here, but she's barely written back. Have you talked to her? Did she say she misses me?*

"What are you *doing,* Tweety?"

I gasp, looking up. Marianna is bending down, frowning at me. "That's MY diary. It's *private.*"

I toss the notebook aside like it's on fire. "I was just looking at how you decorated the cover. I didn't read anything."

Marianna squints. "Liar." She grabs the notebook.

"I forgot my questions for Mom. Don't go snooping through the rest of my stuff while I'm gone."

"Look, don't be mad at me," I say as she crawls back out. "I didn't read anything important."

"Everything I write is important," Marianna says, standing up. "But I'm not mad at you, so relax. Just ask next time, that's all."

Later at home, Mom makes me a grilled cheese sandwich, then she sets her laptop on the kitchen counter and turns it on.

I carry my supper to the living room, take a few bites of my sandwich, then find my diary and work on the cover some more. Shakespeare hops up next to me on the couch and snuggles in. I pet him as he purrs. "Do you miss me when I'm gone, Shakespeare?" I ask.

"Mew," Shakespeare replies, rubbing his cheek against my leg.

"I miss you too," I say. "Tomorrow is Friday, so I have to go away again. I wish I didn't, but it's the only way I get to see Dad. He misses you. He told me so."

Shakespeare cuddles closer. Mom is talking on her phone now. I think it's her lawyer again. ". . . so, are you saying if I agree to his attorney's latest proposal, we can finalize this by Thanksgiving?" There's a pause, then Mom adds, "Okay, good. Let's stick to that plan."

I sigh and open my diary.

Dear Diary,

Marianna caught me lying about Dad working out of town this week. Then she caught me reading her diary. I thought she would be super-mad at me, just like Amber. But she didn't get mad at all. She has lots of questions, just like me. One of them doesn't make sense, though. Something about a big house and a little house. She's always bragging about her big house, but she's never mentioned a little one before.

Mom wants the divorce to get done by Thanksgiving. That's only a couple months away. Then comes Christmas. We always go to G-ma and G-pa's house for the hol-

*idays. Will they let Dad come too? Or is
only Mom invited now? And what about
my birthday? If it's during the week, will I
celebrate with Mom? If it's on the weekend,
will Dad have my party? They always tell
my birthday story together. But Marianna
says even my stories will change now.*

CHAPTER 14

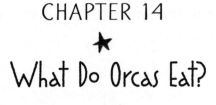

What Do Orcas Eat?

The next day at school, Marianna doesn't ask any more questions about Dad being out of town. And I don't ask any questions about her friend Sasha, who doesn't write to her anymore.

When I sit down by Ruby on Bus #5 after school, Bowtie hovers behind us like a pair of mosquitoes.

"Well, look who's here," Bo says to me. "What's up with you being on my bus again, Byrd?"

"Yeah, what's up with that?" Ty adds.

"Did ya hear me, Byrd?" Bo pokes my shoulder. "What's up?"

Ruby whips a look at Bo. "The *sky*," she snarks. We both giggle.

"I told you already," I say, glancing at Bowtie. "I'm helping my dad with a project."

"What kind of project?" Bo asks.

I don't answer.

"I bet it's a *bird*house," Ty says, snickering. "Big enough for her whole birdbrain family. What's your mom cooking for supper tonight? Fried worms?"

They both crack up.

"You have worms for brains," Ruby says. Then we crack up too.

Ruby and I scrunch down and play with a cootie catcher she made during free time today. She wrote funny fortunes inside it, like *You will be a rock star!* and *You will own a cookie factory!* We ignore Bo and Ty even though they keep chirping like birds and pecking at our hair for bugs, pretending to *eat* them.

Boys.

When the bus comes to my stop, Dad is sitting on the steps of his cabin just like last Friday.

"Hey, Squirt," he says. "What's up?"

"The sky," I reply, sitting down on the step.

Dad chuckles, tousling my hair. "Your mom called a few minutes ago," he says.

"She did? She called you?" My stomach flutters.

Dad nods. "Your grandparents are taking a little trip this weekend. They're swinging through town tomorrow morning. Your mom is wondering if you could have lunch with them. I said fine by me, but I'd have to check with you."

"But it's Saturday tomorrow," I say. "You're in charge of me."

"True, but we can bend the rules as long as everyone agrees."

"Okay, I'll go," I say. "Are you coming too?"

"No," Dad replies. "Just you."

"But why? Don't you want to see G-ma and G-pa?"

Dad starts thumbing a message to Mom. "I wouldn't mind seeing them, but not just yet. We'll all do lunch again, someday. I promise."

When Dad pulls into Mom's driveway the next morning, he doesn't turn off his truck engine or roll down his window to talk to Mom when she comes out of the house. She smiles and waves at us.

Dad gives her a nod, then turns to me. "Have fun, Squirt. Your mom will bring you home this afternoon." He leans over and gives me a quick kiss on my forehead.

"Don't you want to come in and say hi?" I ask, even though I already know the answer.

Dad shakes his head. "See ya later, alligator."

"After a while, crocodile."

G-pa and G-ma come out of the house to hug me. I glance back just in time to see Dad drive away.

Dear Diary,

I saw Mom today even though it's Sat-urday. G-pa and G-ma were here for a visit. We got takeout from Large Marge's and ate at the park. Our picnic table was straight across the lake from Dad's cabin. I told them about my bunk bed, and the little shelf Dad hung on my wall, and the broken storm door, and the yucky toadstools that look like alien brains. That last part made everyone laugh, even Mom. I hadn't heard her laugh like that in a really long time.

After lunch, G-pa and G-ma gave me a present—a little glass unicorn. It's milky white with a shiny gold horn. G-ma said it belonged to Mom when she was a little girl.

I was so excited. I told them I would keep it on my new shelf at Dad's house. They smiled, but in a quiet way. Were they hoping I'd keep the unicorn at Mom's house?

I looked at Mom.

But she just nodded at me and said she liked my plan.

When I got back from lunch, and showed Dad the unicorn, he said it probably means a lot to Mom that it belongs to me now.

I glance over from my bunk bed and see the unicorn on my shelf. She looks happy sitting next to my orca eraser, even though I'm pretty sure an orca would eat a unicorn in real life.

I take out my phone so I can look up the word *unicorn*. But I tap it in wrong and the word *unity* pops up instead.

Unity
- A condition of harmony
- Being in full agreement
- Balance
- Symmetry

Then I look up *symmetry*.

Symmetry
- Two halves that are the same in size, shape, and position
- Balanced proportions
- Beauty of form

Two halves that are the same, I say to myself. Like when Dad cuts an apple sideways and each half has a matching star in the middle. Or that yin-yang thing Marianna is always drawing, with the twin tadpoles. Can it work for families too? Or best friends? If they get divided, do both halves match?

There's a knock on my bedroom door. Dad looks in. "Popcorn?" he asks.

"Sure," I say, setting aside my phone. He hands a popcorn bowl to me, then pats my leg. "You good for now? I've got to finish writing up an expense sheet for a client, then we could play a game or read a book."

"Is the client Marianna's stepdad?" I ask. "She said you were at her house this week."

Dad nods. "I'm his contractor for their new inn."

I frown. "They have an inn? I thought you were fixing their house."

Dad shakes his head. "It used to be a house, but now they're turning it into a bed-and-breakfast. It's in worse shape than Reuben thought, though, so it should keep me busy for a while."

"But, Marianna told me they live there."

"They do," Dad says. "Out back, in a little cottage. Reuben showed it to me. It's cute! You'd like it." He pats my leg again. "Ten minutes, tops, then I'll let you beat me at Scrabble."

I purse my lips. "I'll beat you fair and square," I reply.

Dad laughs. As he turns to leave, he sees my little unicorn and orca sitting on the shelf.

"The unicorn looks good up there," Dad says, glancing from the shelf to me. "But you better keep an eye on the killer whale. They eat unicorns, you know."

"I know," I reply, playing along.

When Dad leaves, I read the definition of *unity* again. Then I draw Marianna's yin-yang tadpoles in my diary. Underneath them I write three words.

Beauty of form

CHAPTER 15

★

Are We in Trouble?

All week, Mom is busy working at the library or doing paperwork at home or talking on the phone with her lawyer. I'm getting good at eating supper from take-out boxes and reading myself bedtime stories.

Marianna keeps bragging to us about having a big party at her house as soon as her mom gets here. How Reuben will cook us a big meal, and we'll eat off flowery china dishes and drink sparkling apple juice from fancy goblets. Then we'll watch movies on their giant screen, and no one will have to sleep on the floor, because her house has so many beds.

The other girls hang on her every word. Mari-anna talks big, but on the inside I know she's the same size as me.

I could tell them the truth. Then maybe Amber would stop treating Marianna like a diva. Maybe she'd want to be my best friend again.

But I know what it feels like to have a big secret you don't want anyone to know. I keep quiet.

When I ride the bus to Dad's house on Friday, Bowtie sits behind Ruby and me again. But this time they don't pick at our hair or tease me about my name. Instead, they show us their dead fly col-lection. I'm not a big fan of dead flies, but as long as they don't throw them at me, I'll pretend I'm interested. I tell them I collect stuff too.

"Like what?" Bo asks.

"Erasers, mostly," I reply. "And unicorns."

"Real ones?" Ty asks.

Bo gives him the elbow. "Don't be a dope, Ty. She means pretend ones. Unicorns ain't real."

"How many do you have?" Ruby asks me.

"Only one so far," I say. "It's made of glass."

"I have one that's made of glass too, and one that's a pillow," Ruby says.

Ty makes a skunk face. "I'd rather collect dead flies."

"My sister's got a bunch of toy ones," Bo says to me. "Unicorns, I mean. She's too big to play with them now. I'll see if I can get one for you. You too, Ruby."

We both smile, surprised. Usually the only thing Bo gives us girls is a snap with a rubber band. "Thanks, Bo!" Ruby and I say.

Bo shrugs, and ducks his eyes. Then he sits back in his seat, messing with his dead fly collection, ears on fire.

When I get home a few minutes later, Dad is inside, making a pot of chili. The cabin smells warm and spicy instead of damp and musty.

Later, when he asks me to carry the trash outside after supper, I'm surprised to see that the broken storm door has glass now. Dad must have fixed it this week. And when I walk across the backyard to the garbage can, the leaves are raked and the grass is mowed. The toadstools are gone.

I read Dad a chapter from my reading book before he tucks me in for the night.

"I've got to meet with a couple people tomorrow morning," he says, tucking in the blankets around me. "You'll have to tag along. Bring some books to read."

"Can I go to the library instead?" I ask. "Mom told me she works this weekend."

"Sure thing," Dad says. "I'll drop you off on the way into town, and pick you up when I'm done."

At the library the next morning, I march in like I'm Marianna Van Den Heuval and shout, "Surprise!"

Mom looks up from the mail she's sorting. "Well, look who's here!" she says, setting down the envelope in her hand and walking around her desk to hug me. She doesn't say anything about my loud voice, or my crooked braids (Dad did my hair this morning), so I know she's really happy to see me.

"Dad has to meet with somebody about fixing

something," I tell her. "He said I could wait here . . . okay?"

"Absolutely okay," Mom replies, hugging me tighter. "You can help me organize the inter-library loan books. A shipment just came in."

Mom and I start going through the stack of books and DVDs on her desk, matching them with the names of people who ordered them from other libraries. Halfway through the pile of books, I pick up one called *All About Sea Glass*.

"Oh, good," Mom says, glancing over as I flip through the pages. "That's the book Marianna has been pester—I mean, *ask*ing—about. She'll be happy it's finally here." Mom smiles to herself as she goes back to work. "*I'm* happy it's finally here."

"Marianna said she and her mom collect sea glass," I say. "They make jewelry out of it. Only now they can't, because there are no oceans in Oak Hill. And her mom still isn't here."

"I'm sure that's very hard on Marianna," Mom says. "Would you like to bring the book to her? It might make her feel more at home."

I close the book slowly, thinking through Mom's suggestion. If I take the book to her, she'll know that I know her secret. But would that be a bad thing or a good thing? If she lets me in on her secret, will it make her little cottage feel more like home?

I look at Mom. "Okay, I'll bring the book to Marianna."

"Do you know which house?" Mom asks.

I nod. "It's the big one, just around the corner. But Dad's supposed to meet me here," I say, tucking the book under my arm.

"If he shows up," Mom says, "I'll text you to come back."

I get to Marianna's cul-de-sac a few minutes later. Her house really does look tall enough to be a diva's castle. It's brick, with a big white porch that wraps around one side. As I walk toward the front steps, a lacy curtain flutters in one of the downstairs windows. I catch a glimpse of a swinging ponytail and hear someone squawk, *"Oh. Em. Gee!"*

The front door flies open. Marianna jumps out onto the porch in her stocking feet and pulls the door closed behind her. "What are you doing here, Tweety?!"

"Special delivery," I reply, holding up the sea glass book. "It came in at the library this morning. My mom thought you'd like to have it right away."

"Oh," Marianna says, snatching the book from me. "Thanks." She hugs it to her chest and shifts from one stocking foot to the other. "Well, then. Good-bye."

She reaches behind her for the doorknob and starts to back her way inside.

"*Um*Do you want to show me your new house?" I ask.

Marianna swallows. Her throat clicks. "Yes, but . . . it's just . . ." She looks over her shoulder. I wait for her to decide.

"Okay." She hugs the book tighter, like a shield. "I'll give you a quick tour. Take off your shoes. Don't touch anything."

Marianna opens the front door and peeks in

like she's checking to see if the coast is clear, then lets me follow her inside.

"This is my grand entryway," she says in a queenly voice.

I kick off my sneakers, looking at the huge staircase with a carved wooden railing. But some of the fancy-patterned wallpaper is peeling at the edges. The carpeting on the staircase is threadbare. When I touch the wooden railing, it wobbles. A small table holds an empty flower vase and a book with gold letters on its cover.

Our Guests

Marianna puts the sea glass book on top of the guest book, then she picks up my shoes and places them neatly on a shoe mat next to a pair of cute polka-dot flats. They look the same size as my sneakers.

"Through here is the main parlor." Marianna continues the tour, leading me into a cozy room. There's a fireplace, but it looks like it hasn't been used for a long time. Moving boxes are stacked next to it. *Charlotte's Web* is lying open on the only chair in the room.

"Hey, my mom and I are reading that book too," I say.

"I'm reading it to myself," Marianna replies.

One of the moving boxes is open and I see a picture of Reuben on top. He's wearing a suit and tie, standing next to a short woman with a pretty smile. The woman has on a white dress with a wreath of flowers in her hair. "Is that your mom?" I ask, picking up the picture.

Marianna nods. "It's from their wedding."

"She's pretty," I say.

"I know," Marianna replies.

I give her a sideways glance. "When did you say she's moving here?"

"Soon," Marianna says, taking the picture from me and setting it on the fireplace mantel. "She promised."

She pulls me away.

"Over here is the dining room." Marianna walks me into a room with a long table and lots of chairs.

"Wow, you could sit in a different place every day of the week!" I say.

Marianna rushes on with her tour. "That's the kitchen," she says, pointing to a door across the dining room. "Reuben is cooking a new recipe. Don't worry if you smell something funny."

I take a sniff, but all I smell is something sweet and delicious. I hear kettles clanking and music playing, and Reuben singing along with the song, not very well. "Should we tell him I'm here?" I ask.

"No," Marianna replies. "He doesn't like to be disturbed when he's cooking."

I look around the room again and see another closed door with a sign hanging on the doorknob.

Private Entrance

"Where does that door lead?" I ask.

"That's not important, Tweety." Marianna takes my arm. "Come with me." She pulls me back through the living room to the staircase in the entryway. The steps creak as we walk up them.

"Is this the way to your bedroom?" I ask.

"*Mmm-hmm*," Marianna replies.

When we get to the landing at the top of the stairs, Marianna opens a little cupboard and takes out a set of keys. Walking up to the first door that lines the narrow hallway, she tries to fit one of the keys into its lock. When it won't go, she mutters something under her breath, then tries another key. And *another*.

This would be a good time to tell her I know this isn't her bedroom. But then she'll know I've been pretending. Instead, I ask, "Are you afraid of robbers?"

"I'm not afraid of anything," Marianna snips, choosing a fourth key on the ring and wiggling it into the lock.

"It's just that, most kids in Oak Hill don't lock their bedrooms," I explain. "Most grown-ups don't either. My dad doesn't even lock his truck when he runs into the grocery store."

Marianna glances up. "For reals?"

I nod. "You're not in Seattle anymore."

Marianna turns the key. The lock catches. The door swings open.

"Welcome to my bedroom," Marianna says, glancing back toward the staircase. "Remember, don't touch anything."

She steps aside to let me in, but I don't move. "Are you sure we shouldn't tell Reuben I'm here?"

"No, I told you he's busy!" Marianna nudges me through the doorway.

The room is empty, except for more unpacked boxes and a huge bed with no covers on it. "Rueben is washing my sheets today," Marianna quickly explains.

A door closes downstairs. A moment later, footsteps creak on the staircase.

Marianna stiffens.

"Mare Bear?" a man's voice calls out. "Are you playing upstairs again?"

Marianna flies to the bedroom door and slams it shut, keys jangling in the lock on the other side. She leans against it, locks eyes with me, and puts a finger to her lips. "Shhh . . . !"

"I knew we shouldn't be in here!"

Marianna leans harder. The door pushes open.

Reuben pokes in from the hallway. "Hello,

Wren!" he says. "I didn't know we had company!"

Marianna turns to glare at her stepdad. "Go away, Reuben! You're bothering us!"

Reuben opens the door wider. "You know the rules, Mare Bear," he says. "No playing in the guest rooms."

Marianna's cheeks turn bright red. She crosses her arms over her chest, scowling.

"Are we in trouble?" I ask.

Reuben turns to me. "Not at all, Wren. I just don't want you girls tripping over loose flooring, or stepping on a nail while we fix the place up. Did Marianna tell you? We're turning my boyhood home into an inn! This will be one of the guest rooms. It's been our dream for a long time."

"*Your* dream!" Marianna shouts at Reuben. "Not mine!" She storms out of the room. A minute later, a door slams beneath us.

Reuben's shoulders sag. He runs his long fingers through his thin hair. Then he looks at me. "I take it Marianna is still pretending that we live in the big house?"

I nod. "I think she's pretending about her mom too. She keeps saying she will be here soon."

Reuben sighs. "That was the original plan, but things have changed. Sara won't be arriving for another month. Maybe two. Marianna is having trouble accepting that fact." He pulls the ring of keys from the door lock. "It's been hard on her, leaving her family and friends in Seattle to move here with me. Her mother and I thought it best if she had a chance to make new friends before the start of the school year, but perhaps we should have waited."

Reuben puts the keys in his pocket, then smiles kindly at me. "We'll give Marianna a moment to catch her breath, eh, Wren? Then I'll serve you two a treat. Crêpes suzette! It's my latest creation for the inn's menu!"

Reuben tells me all about his plans for the inn as we head downstairs. And how he and Marianna, and soon her mom, live in the carriage house out back, which is where they kept horse buggies in the olden days, but now it's fixed up for people.

"There's still lots of work to be done . . ." Reuben says as we walk into the dining room. "I'm grateful your dad is helping me. I had hoped to be further along with everything, but with Sara still in Seattle, we are a bit behind. Marianna misses her mother terribly, of course. She misses her father too. The smallest things set her off, lately . . ."

I listen, realizing Marianna hasn't seen her parents since the beginning of summer. At least I get to see my mom and dad every week, even if it's one at a time.

"I hope you can be patient with her, Wren," Reuben says. "She could use a good friend like you."

A timer starts beeping in the kitchen. "OhEm-Gee!" Reuben exclaims. "I completely forgot about my orange sauce!" Quickly, he points toward the *Private Entrance* door. "Straight through there, Wren. You'll find Marianna in the cottage out back. Can't miss it!"

Reuben rushes off to the kitchen.

I walk over to the door and open it. A vine-covered trellis marks the beginning of a path that leads to a little house hidden behind a tall hedge in the backyard. I step through the doorway and hurry down the path. Reuben might think that Marianna could use a friend like me, but maybe it's me who could use a friend like *her*.

CHAPTER 16

★

Why Don't We Eat at the Table Anymore?

Marianna glances up from a corner desk in her bedroom when I peek in a few minutes later. It was easy to find her room because the cottage isn't much bigger than Dad's cabin.

"Oh," she says casually. "It's you, Tweety." Then she goes back to drawing in a notebook, like she doesn't care that I know her secrets now.

"Um, Reuben told me about your mom not getting to move here for a while."

Marianna shrugs. "It's no big deal."

"It would be a big deal to me," I say. "I had

to be away from my parents for two months this summer."

Marianna looks at me again, starts to say something, then stops. Turning back to her drawing, she says, "So now you know the truth. I don't have a big house or a big bedroom. I sleep in a mouse nest."

I look around her bedroom. The only furniture in here is the little desk, a kid-sized bed, and a small dresser. Clothes are crowded on hangers inside a cubbyhole closet. Shoes, toys, and books are piled in boxes on the floor.

"It's not so small," I say, trying to sound upbeat.

Marianna looks at me and rolls her eyes. "If there's one thing I *hate*, Tweety, it's a liar."

I sigh. "Well, all right, it *is* small. But that doesn't make it bad. Like my mom says, big things can come in small packages."

Marianna huffs and shakes her head. But a moment later she gives me a cautious glance. "Do you really think my room is okay?"

I nod, walking over to her. "It's like a book nook. You can imagine it as big as you want." I pick up a framed picture from her desk. The photo is of Marianna with her mom and a man with a ponytail that's as long as hers.

"Is this your dad?" I ask.

Marianna nods. "Richard Van Den Heuval, but everyone calls him Van. He's an artist, just like my mom."

"He looks nice."

"He is."

We hear the front door to the cottage open and a moment later Reuben ducks in. "Room service!" he sings cheerfully, setting a tray of food on Marianna's bed. "Crêpes suzette, apple juice, and coffee with lots of cream and sugar, just the way you like it, Mare Bear. Sorry about the orange sauce. It got a little . . . well done. But the ice cream is *exceptionnelle*. I churned it myself this morning!"

I look at the big scoops of vanilla ice cream melting over a platter of crispy golden crepes. "Yum!" I say. "Thank you!"

Reuben smiles at me. "*Pas de quoi,* Wren," he says. "That's French for 'Don't mention it.'"

Marianna pushes back from her desk and

stands up. "You made me cry in front of my friend," she says to Reuben. "Don't expect a thank-you from me."

"I never expect one," Reuben replies, "I only hope. I'm sorry if I startled you girls earlier. I don't mind that you play in the inn, I only ask that you check with me first."

Marianna crosses her arms and stares at her polka-dot shoes. "We were only looking around," she mumbles. "I didn't let Wren touch anything."

I nod. "That's true. She didn't."

Reuben's eyes crinkle with a smile. "Dig in, girls. Your crepes are getting cold."

Marianna and I sit crisscross applesauce on her little bed with the tray of food between us.

"Reuben's nice," I say.

Marianna pauses. "I know.

"Promise me you won't tell the other girls the truth, Tweety?" she asks.

"I promise," I reply.

"I didn't mean to lie about anything," Marianna tells me as we eat. "Amber and the other girls biked by when the movers were here this summer. They thought I was moving into the big house, so I just played along. Then we got to be friends and it seemed harder to tell them the truth than to keep pretending. Besides, I thought my mom would take my side when she got here and we would all live in the big house instead of this dinky cottage. But then she couldn't come right away. And Reuben kept unpacking boxes and making his plans. I felt like I didn't have a say in anything."

I eat quietly while Marianna talks. It's easier to listen to her when she isn't using her teacher voice.

Marianna sets aside her plate and picks up a book. "Want to see my diary?"

While I eat a second helping, she sips coffee and shows me her favorite pages. Each one has more pictures than words—drawings of seagulls flying over a beach; her mom picking up shells and sea glass; her dad painting at an easel; a girl with red hair flying a kite.

"Is that your friend Sasha?" I ask, pointing to the girl.

Marianna nods. "I drew it on my last birthday. Reuben gave me the kite for a present."

After we finish eating, Marianna takes the tray back to the kitchen for Reuben. I flip through more pages in her diary. Mountains. Sailboats. Orcas. Toward the back is a drawing of a girl with a dark brown braid, dark blue eyes, and orange sneakers, just like mine. I smile when I see *Tweety* written on the girl's shirt.

I walk over to Marianna's desk and pick up another selfie of her family. Both of her parents have big smiles. Marianna is sandwiched between them, smiling the biggest of all. She said her parents got divorced a long time ago, but this photo looks brand-new. Marianna is even wearing the sparkly Seattle shirt she had on at Family Night. They must have taken this picture right before she moved here.

I set the picture down, wondering if I'll ever get to be in the middle of a family sandwich again.

When I get back to the library later, Mom is on the phone. Right away I know she's talking to

Dad. I can tell by the way she snips her words like she's trimming my bangs.

"Yes. No. Sure. Drop it off next week."

Mom glances up and sees me. "Wren's here. Yes, of course." She clicks off her phone and smiles at me. "Your dad says hi."

"Hi," I say to the blank screen.

"He's running late and so I offered to bring you to his place, when I'm done in an hour." She starts typing on her computer. "Did you eat? There's some cold pizza in my lunch box."

"I'm not hungry," I say, sitting down on an extra desk chair. "Reuben made crepes and vanilla ice cream. It was *délicieuse*. Marianna told me that's French for delicious. We got to use nice dishes too, like G-ma keeps in her china hutch. How come we never eat fancy food anymore?"

"I have to work extra hours now, Wren, you know that."

"Yes, but I still *Need. To. Eat.*"

Mom looks at me over the top of her glasses. "I'm not crazy about your attitude."

"I'm not crazy about cold pizza."

Mom ignores me, but I keep going. "We don't eat fancy food even when you aren't working late. It's always whatever is in the fridge. And we never sit at the table."

"That simply isn't true," Mom replies, fingers flying over her keyboard.

"It *is* true. We always eat at the kitchen counter. At Dad's place, we always sit on the couch. Don't divorced people believe in chairs and placemats?"

Mom stops typing.

I sink down and cross my arms.

We sit there in noisy silence for a minute. Then Mom takes off her glasses and pinches the bridge of her nose, like she's trying not to sneeze. When she starts to speak, her words are chopped with tears. "I . . . I . . . just . . . I just can't . . ." Then the tears really start to come.

I've seen Mom cry before. When she hit that deer with her car. When Dad gave her a diamond necklace for Christmas. When her favorite uncle died. But Dad was always there to stop her tears. Now it's only me.

I start pulling tissues out of the box Mom keeps on her desk. One . . . three . . . five . . . how many is enough? I take two more and push them all into her hands. "Please don't cry. I'm sorry I complained about the food."

Mom takes the heap of tissues and wipes her eyes. "You have a right to complain," she says a moment later. "It's true. I don't cook like I used to and we rarely eat at the table. Your dad and I were sitting there when we decided to get a divorce. I don't like being reminded of that conversation."

My chest tightens. "That's just like my koala bear shirt," I say quietly. "The one that matches Amber's. It's my favorite, but I was wearing it on the day you told me about the divorce. I've tried to wear it since then, but it doesn't feel right, so I stuffed it at the bottom of my drawer."

Mom's eyes fill with fresh tears. "I wondered what happened to that shirt." She pulls me into her arms. Now she's using my shoulder for a tissue, but I don't mind.

A minute later, I pull back and look at Mom. "I don't want us to be divorced, Mom. I miss Dad all week, and I miss you all weekend."

"I know, honey," she says. "I miss being all together sometimes too. And I'm sorry we have to go through it. But we *will* get through it, okay? All of us. You. Me. Your dad."

The door opens. A group of older boys come in. One of them is Ruby's brother. I recognize him from the bus.

Mom blows her nose. "Time to get back to work," she says, throwing away the tissues. "Then I'll drive you to your dad's place."

I nod.

She kisses the top of my head. "Thanks," she says.

"For what?" I ask.

"For the tissues. And for reminding me that it's not good to pretend to be more pulled together than I actually am. That it's okay to admit that things are hard right now. I'll think on that. Besides, pretending takes a lot of work."

The next day, I think a lot about what Mom said about pretending. I think about telling Marianna the truth. That I've been pretending about my family too. But I don't know how.

CHAPTER 17

★

Why Is Mom Wearing a Ring?

When Monday comes, I don't say anything to the other girls about Marianna's cottage. At recess, Amber keeps peppering her with questions about the big party she's going to have. *When will it be? How much longer?? Why can't we have it right away???*

I start a game of horses to change the subject. Marianna gives me a relieved smile, and even plays along. She tells us her horse is the color of beach sand. She names her Seattle. All week, Marianna wants to play horses at recess.

Marianna and I don't talk much on the way to

the library after school, but that's not a bad thing. Friends don't always need to fill up the quiet spaces with lots of words.

"Are you coming inside today?" I ask Marianna when we get to the library steps on Thursday.

"Of course, Tweety, don't I always?" she replies.

When I open the door, I see that Dad is there, talking with Mom.

I freeze in the doorway. I haven't seen Mom and Dad together in the same room since Family Night at school. It's weird how something that used to be so ordinary seems like the biggest deal in the world now.

In less time than it takes Marianna to ask, "Why the freeze face, Tweety? It's just your mom and dad," my brain kicks up a zillion questions.

Why is Dad here?

Did Mom call him after she cried on Saturday?

Did Dad stop by to give her a hug and tell her everything would be okay?

Why is Mom holding a little velvety box?

Ohmygosh, is that a new ring on her finger??

Did Dad just give it to her???

Does he want to be married again????
Does Mom?????

"Dad!" I blurt, flying across the room to him.

"Hey, Squirt!" Dad catches me up in a big hug.

"Hi, girls!" Mom says cheerfully. She waves Marianna over to us and the new ring on her finger sparkles under the fluorescent ceiling lights. Her old wedding ring was a plain gold band. *This* ring has a pretty red stone. Mom's favorite color!

"Hello, Mrs. Byrd," Marianna replies. She opens her tote bag and pulls out a picture book called *Winter in Wisconsin.* "Reuben checked this out for me. I told him it's for little kids, but I read it anyway. Did you know people around here sculpt *actual* castles out of snow? Where I come from, we make them out of sand." She tilts her hips. "I might try it with snow this year."

Mom smiles and reaches for the book. The ring glimmers on her hand.

I beam at Dad as he sets me down again. "I like the new ring you gave Mom! The old one was so plain. This one is a lot better!"

I look back and forth between Dad and Mom,

waiting for them to tell me that we are going to be a family again. But they just stand there, making freeze faces at each other.

"Oh dear," Mom says, touching the ring. She wiggles it over her knuckle. "It's not what you think, Wren. This ring belonged to my grandmother. It got mixed in with your dad's things. He was just returning it to me."

Mom puts the ring back in the little velvety box and closes the lid.

My heart sinks to my stomach.

To my knees.

To my sneakers.

Dumb little bird, I say to myself, turning away. *Mom and Dad aren't getting back together. They're still just dividing up their stuff.* I squeeze my eyes shut. Tears creep out.

A hand touches my shoulder. "Squirt, you didn't think your mom and I—?"

I shake off Dad's hand and jerk away. "Don't call me that!" I shout at him. "I hate *Squirt*! I'm sick of '*your* mom' and '*your* dad'!" Tears flood my eyes.

Dad kneels next to me. "Wren," he says. "Wren . . ."

I collapse against his shoulder and sob.

Suddenly, Mom is there with a handful of tissues, wiping my eyes, my cheeks, my chin. Then she puts her arms around me too. We stay like that, crouched together until my sobs turn into words again. "I just want . . . want us . . . to go home."

Dad looks at Mom. "Maybe I should take her back to your place?"

Mom nods. "I'll meet you there."

Mom and Dad stand up.

I realize Marianna is still here.

"I better go," she says quietly. "See you at school, Wren?"

I nod, feeling too numb to talk.

Too numb to look at her.

Almost too numb to feel her squeeze my arm as she brushes past me and heads out the door.

On our way home, I try to make a nook for myself in the front seat by scrunching down and covering my head with my jacket.

I can barely hear Dad when he asks, "Do you want to talk about it?"

"No," I say through the fabric.

"Do you want to wait in the truck while I pick up supper for you two?"

"Yes."

"How about I run a bubble bath when we get to your mom's?"

"Okay."

Later, while I'm in the tub, which is the most private of private times in a girl's life, Mom peeks in to check on me. "I'm home now, Wren, are you okay?"

"Yes."

"Are you sure?"

"YES!!"

I plug my nose and dunk below the bubbles.

I can't believe I bawled like a baby in front of Marianna. How could I think my parents were getting back together?

When I come up for air, Shakespeare is standing on the edge of the tub.

"Mew?" he says.

I reach up to scratch his chest, fresh tears filling my eyes. They roll down my cheeks and off my chin.

"If Dad were living here, the crybaby scene never would have happened," I tell him. "They wouldn't be acting like I'm made of glass. I could be with you every day of the week."

Shakespeare sits down, listening. His tail tips a shampoo bottle into the water. It floats like a little island in a sudsy sea.

"I could call Amber and we would plan a sleepover for this weekend, just like we always used to do. Remember how we would dress you up in old doll clothes and pretend you were our baby brother? It felt like we were a real family even though it was just pretend. Now I have to pretend we are a real family all the time."

When Shakespeare finally hops down and slips out the door, I hug my knees until the bathwater turns cold. Then I open the drain and my tears wash away in the sudsy sea.

Dad is gone when I get downstairs from my bath. Mom is in the kitchen, talking on her phone. I'm not hungry, but I grab a take-out box and a plastic fork from the counter anyway. Then I shuffle to the dining room in my slippers and crawl under the table. Shakespeare winds his way in through the chair legs.

Sitting down and closing my eyes, I imagine myself smaller and smaller, until I'm the size of my cat. When I open my eyes again, the table is my little house. The chairs are the doors and windows.

Shakespeare curls up next to me.

"Are you hiding?"

I look past Shakespeare and see Mom's stocking feet. She leans over and looks at me, a take-out container and a paper cup of coffee in her hands.

"No," I reply. "I'm pretending."

Mom moves a chair. "Is there room for me?"

"Really?"

Without answering, she crawls under the table too, scooting in next to me and trying to bend her legs in a yoga move.

It takes her a while, but when she's all settled, she smiles at me. "Cozy."

Mom's never sat in one of my nooks.

Spreading out some napkins, we start eating. Quietly.

Even though we're sitting on the floor, using plastic silverware and take-out boxes for bowls, Mom doesn't make believe it's a picnic. I'm glad because it's too hard to always pretend that everything is happily-ever-after when it isn't.

The pocket on Mom's blazer chirps. She sets down her salad, pulls out her phone, and checks the screen. "It's your dad," she says, setting the phone on the floor. "I'll put him on speaker."

"Hi, Dad," I say.

"Hey, Squir—Wren." With him on speaker, it's almost like he's sitting here with us. "What's up?" he asks.

"The table," I say. "Mom and I are sitting under it. I guess you are too."

"Cozy!" Dad says. "I was just thinking, I haven't asked you any good questions in a while. Got time for a quick round?"

"Shoot," I reply.

"Okay," Dad says, thinking for a moment before he begins.

"Was that a grizzly bear I saw lounging in your bedroom earlier?"

"No, it was a polar bear."

"Heh, heh. Good one. Did capuchin monkeys invade your school today and hold the principal hostage?"

Giggle. "No."

"Did you raise your hand during math class?"

"Yes."

"Attagirl! Did you ace your spelling quiz?"

"Not yet, but I will tomorrow."

"How many boyfriends do you have these days?"

"Yuck. Zero."

"How many erasers, then?"

"Fifty."

"Wow! That's a lot. Do you know how much I love you, Wren?"

"How much?"

"More than fifty times fifty times fifty again."

"Wow! That's a lot."

"Yep. And your mom loves you just as much, got that?"

"Okay."

"Done," Dad says.

"But that was only a few questions," I say.

"It's a good place to stop for now. We'll have more this weekend. Don't forget to ride the bus to my place."

I roll my eyes. "I'm not a baby anymore, Dad. You and Mom don't have to keep reminding me."

I hear Dad smile. "Got it."

"And . . . I don't actually mind *Squirt*."

"Didn't believe it for a minute."

I breathe a sigh of relief. "Bye for now."

"Over and out."

"Grizzly bears and capuchin monkeys?" Mom says as she tucks her phone away. "Your dad has added new material to his repertoire." She takes a sip of coffee, then smiles. A real smile.

"Mom? Can I ask you a question?"

"Of course," she replies.

"Will we ever be happy again?"

She studies my face for a moment, like it's a line from a poem she doesn't want to forget. I think she's trying not to cry again, but she doesn't look away.

"I know things are different now," Mom says. "I wish *different* was the same as *happy,* but it's not."

I stop chewing.

"Someday we'll be happy," she tells me. "But for now, I'd say we're happi*er*."

"Happier-ever-after?" I ask.

Mom nods and gently rests her forehead against mine. "Happier-ever-after."

CHAPTER 18
★
What If...?

"Marianna must wonder why I got so upset," I tell Shakespeare that night. He tucks himself into a little ball next to me on the bed. I pick up my blue notebook.

Dear Diary,
   Some new stuff has happened since the last time I wrote in here. I found out Marianna was lying about living in a big house. But instead of being mad, Marianna seemed relieved. Mom says pretending is

hard work. But I think telling the truth is
even harder.

How can I tell my friends I've been lying
to them all this time? I don't even know
where to start.

Shakespeare stretches. His tail curls around my
phone.

Hmmm.

How do I admit a lie? I type into my phone.

A list appears on my screen. Only four steps.
Maybe this won't be as hard as I thought.

1. Prepare the other person for the truth.
Warning the other person may help to lessen the
blow that you have been lying to them. Start by
saying: "There's something important I want to
tell you. We need to have a serious talk."

I turn toward Shakespeare. "There's something
important I have to tell you," I say, practicing.
"We need to have a serious talk."

Shakespeare looks up from his lick bath. I say
the words again. "There's something important I
have to . . ."

Already my throat aches with tears. I skip ahead to the next step.

2. Choose a quiet place and time of day to talk.
Pick a location that is free from distractions and interruptions.

"Our classroom is too busy," I reason. "And girls are always coming in and out of the restrooms." I'll have to pick a spot on the playground during recess. Maybe the sandbox? Hardly anyone plays there anymore. But what if Amber won't meet up with me?

I sigh and move on to Step 3.

3. Give a detailed description of the lie.
Explain why you didn't tell the truth. Don't try to downplay things. Let the other person decide for themselves if your lie will have big or little consequences.

My stomach flip-flops. This feels like the hardest part. We've never lied to each other before.

4. Apologize for lying.
You may need to apologize several times, or offer a token gift, so the other person knows you are serious about making amends.

What if Amber won't accept my apology, no matter how many times I say it? What if the other girls think I'm a terrible person? Who will I play with at recess? Where will I sit at lunch?

I toss aside my phone and curl into a ball on my bed.

Shakespeare rubs his face against mine.

How many *sorry*s are enough?

CHAPTER 19

★

Do You Want to Play with Us?

The next morning, when everyone is putting away their stuff in the coatroom, Marianna doesn't ask me any questions about what happened at the library. She doesn't call me Crybaby either. I'm still just Tweety to her.

And when I come back from bringing the milk crate to the lunchroom after milk break, there is a new eraser on my chair. It's a pineapple with pokey green spikes on top. Picking it up, I see that the bottom of the pineapple is rubbed down and there are pencil smudges on it. I look at Marianna.

She must use this eraser a lot. It's not an orca, but I bet it's her favorite.

"Thanks," I say, sitting down. "I have three apples, two strawberries, and a banana in my eraser collection, but I don't have a pineapple. And, thanks for not telling everyone what happened at the library yesterday."

"You don't have to thank me. We're even," Marianna says. "Besides, I never blab the big things."

"Thanks anyway," I say.

"You're welcome anyway," she replies.

I face forward in my chair and start to take out my pencil box so I can put the pineapple eraser inside, but Marianna taps my shoulder first. "Oh, and Tweety? *FYI,* I didn't give you that eraser."

I turn around. "Then who did?"

"I don't know. I didn't see."

I wonder if it was Ruby. But I can't think too much about it, because I'm too busy worrying about telling Amber the truth. I practice my lines, over and over in my head. When recess comes, I go outside by myself, and I keep walking until my feet take me to where Amber is talking to Marianna.

"*Um*Awkward silence," I say.

"Tweety," Marianna says. "What's up?"

"I need to talk to Amber. Um, I mean, there's something I have to say. Something important."

Amber gives me a look. "Okay, go ahead."

"But . . ." I start to say.

I have my line all ready, but what comes out is, "I didn't go to Mount Rushmore this summer."

"*That's* what you wanted to tell me?" Amber looks confused. "What are you talking about, Wren?"

"Amber, there are things I haven't told you. . . . Big things."

"Big things?"

Marianna leans in. "Go ahead, Tweety. We're listening."

I look at Amber and try to remember which step comes next. Everything is getting mixed up. "I didn't call you all summer. And I'm so sorry."

"I already know that."

This is not coming out right. I was supposed to save the apology for the end. I keep going.

"But there's a reason I didn't call. I was afraid . . .

if I told you the truth . . . then all the awful stuff would spill out and nothing would ever be the same again."

Amber sucks in her breath like she just got a paper cut. "*What* would never be the same?"

I grip the pineapple eraser in my hand. I thought it would make me feel braver, carrying something with me, and the pineapple was the first thing I saw in my desk. "My dad moved out this summer. He had to because my parents are getting a divorce. That's why I had to go away."

"Oh no!" Amber exclaims. "I can't believe it!"

Marianna doesn't say anything, but she nods, like it all makes sense.

"But, Wren," Amber says, "it's been weeks since school started and you never said anything!"

"I know. When we got to school, everything just got more and more complicated."

Amber crosses her arms. "It doesn't seem that complicated to me."

"I just felt so confused. Over the summer, I had all these big questions and no answers. And then when we got to school, and nobody seemed to know—not even Ms. Little—I thought: What would happen if I just didn't tell anyone anything? What if my parents get back together? What's the point of telling the truth if it's only temporary?" I look at the eraser in my hand, blinking away the sting in my eyes. "You were suddenly best friends with Marianna. And I thought, what if I tell you the truth and you never speak to me again? I'm so sorry, Amber."

Marianna squeezes my arm. "It's okay, Tweety," she says.

But Amber just stands there, staring at the eraser in my hand.

The list said it might help to give the other person a gift. I hold out the pineapple eraser to Amber. "I'm really sorry," I tell her again.

Amber shifts. Then she says, "Wren, I gave you that pineapple eraser."

My eyes go wide. "You did?"

Amber nods.

"OhEmGee," Marianna whispers. "This is so yin-yang."

"I wanted to make you a friendship bracelet

last night," Amber tells me, "but I didn't have any orange gum wrappers. That's your favorite color now, right? I saw it on your *All About Me!* poster, plus most of your notebooks are orange this year, and so is your pencil box and your new sneakers. Nobody in my house had any good gum wrappers to make a bracelet, and it was too late to go to the store, but then my mom told me pineapples are a symbol of friendship, so—"

"I knew that," Marianna interrupts. "Reuben is bananas for pineapples."

"So Slate ran to the pantry and came back with a can of pineapple for you." Amber laughs a little. "Then Ivory disappeared to our room and brought back the pineapple eraser. It was beat up, but she still made me trade *five* of my best jellies for it. What else could I do? I really wanted to give you something because . . . the thing is . . . I miss you, Wren."

I gulp. "You do?"

"I bawled *All. Summer.* I thought you didn't like me anymore. I'm sorry about your mom and dad and everything, but I'm *So. Glad.* We're still friends!"

Amber takes my hand and squeezes it super-tight. The pineapple pokes my fingers, but I don't mind. I squeeze her hand back even tighter.

Marianna clears her throat.

We look at her.

"This is so awkward, Am," she says, "but *I've* got a big secret to tell you too."

"What is it?" Amber asks.

Marianna purses her lips. "You won't believe this, but I don't actually live in a big house. I live in a little cottage behind it. It's even smaller than your house, Am! Tweety saw it the other day. And there's something else I need to tell *both* of you . . ."

Marianna looks from Amber to me. "My mom isn't moving here right away. She promised she would, but sometimes promises get broken. And, the truth is, I only have one best friend in Seattle. At least, I did. I don't think we are best friends anymore."

Marianna ducks her eyes.

I reach over and take her hand too. Amber takes the other one.

We find Phoebe and Eleanor by the swings and Marianna tells them the truth about her house and her mom. Then I tell them the truth about the divorce.

"That's why I have to ride the bus after school on Fridays," I explain. "My dad is living in a cabin on the other side of the lake. I stay with him on the weekends."

"Ohmygosh!" Eleanor says. "That's such a bummer, Wren. My aunt and uncle got one of those. A divorce, I mean."

Phoebe nods. "So did my mom's friend. She had to sell their house and move into a tiny apartment."

"But a cabin sounds like fun!" Eleanor continues. "We could pretend it's the olden days and we're pioneer girls!"

Phoebe starts pumping on her swing. "Our

horses would love that! We could get your dad to build us a stable!"

"That's silly," Marianna says. "We can build a pretend stable by ourselves. We can build a whole *castle*, if we want to. *I'll* be the queen."

I hear a snort-laugh and look toward the twisty slide. Ruby is sitting at the top of it, shaking her head at Marianna.

Marianna squints at Ruby. "What's so funny, Ruby Red Punch? Don't you think I would make a good queen?"

Ruby snickers. "A drama queen, maybe."

Marianna squints harder.

I smile at Ruby. "Do you want to play with us?" I call to her.

Ruby grins. "I'll be right down." Then she pushes off and twists down the slide.

"Fine, she can play with us," Marianna says as Ruby walks over and stands next to me. "But she'll have to wait her turn." Marianna grabs the last empty swing, backs up, and takes off, flying.

CHAPTER 20

★

What's the Definition of <u>Family</u>?

When I get to Dad's place after school later, I take the pineapple eraser from my backpack and set it next to the orca and unicorn. Then I step back and look at my collections. Even though I don't want to live in two places, maybe it doesn't have to be a bad thing.

Later that night, Dad runs a bath for me. I sit and soak in the bubbles while he puts away groceries and gets supper ready.

Plugging my nose, I dunk down and imagine I'm a deep-sea diver, searching for sunken ships and hidden treasure. But it's dark under the ocean. And there are scary sharks and creepy squids hiding behind every reef and boulder. So I take a breath of air, then imagine Amber, Phoebe, Eleanor, Ruby, and Marianna, diving down with me, so we can be scared and creeped out together.

When I come up for air again, Shakespeare is sitting on the edge of the tub.

"Mew?" he says to me.

"Shakespeare!" I cry out in surprise. "What are you doing here?"

I reach over to pet him, but he jumps down and slips out the bathroom door.

"Dad!" I shout. "Shakespeare is here!"

Dad pokes in. "Yep. So is your mom."

Quickly, I get out of the tub, dry off, and pull on some clothes. When I get out to the kitchen, Mom is sitting at the table with Dad. They are both holding cups of coffee. A pizza box is between them.

"I thought it might be nice to have supper together for a change," Mom says.

I walk over to the table and give her a hug. She holds on for a long time.

When she finally lets me go again, Shakespeare is there, purring and rubbing a figure eight around my legs.

"Thanks for bringing him along," I say to Mom, picking up my cat.

Mom reaches over and pets him too. "If you like, I thought he could spend the night."

I give Mom a big smile. Then I look at Dad. "Is that okay?"

"As long as he earns his keep," Dad says. "I saw a mouse this morning."

Mom tenses, but she doesn't say anything.

"Let's eat!" Dad says, opening the pizza box.

I nab a piece of pepperoni for Shakespeare.

"Wren," Mom says, stopping me as I'm about to feed it to him. "Not at the table."

I set Shakespeare on the floor. He curls up under my chair. I sit down and sneak the pepperoni to him.

"Did I hear on the news today that an asteroid penetrated the atmosphere and landed in Pickerel Lake?" Dad asks, dishing up pizza for us.

Mom rolls her eyes and takes the plate he passes to her.

I giggle. "No!"

"Huh," Dad says. "I thought for sure that's what they said."

Mom clears her throat and looks at me. "How did you do on your spelling quiz today?"

"Good!" I say. "Eight right, two wrong. Ms. Little says we should emphasize the positive."

Mom smiles, pleased. She pours me a glass of milk. "Would you like to have a sleepover sometime with your friends? It's been a while."

I pull the glass away from my mouth so fast, milk dribbles down my chin. "We were just talking about that at recess today—me, Amber, Phoebe, Eleanor, Ruby, and Marianna! Everyone wants to see my cabin. We're going to build a pretend stable for our invisible horses down by the lake. Marianna wants to build a castle too so she can rule the world."

"Let me know if you need any help," Dad puts in. "I specialize in pretend stables and aristocratic castles."

I grin even though I'm not sure what *aristocratic* means. I'll have to look it up. "When can I have the sleepover? Next weekend?"

Mom and Dad look at each other for a moment. "She could have it at my place next Friday night," Dad offers.

"It's not just your place now, it's mine too." I glance at Mom. She smiles.

"Roger that," Dad says. "Well, you could have it at *your cabin* or your *other* house across the lake. I'm happy to have it here, but there's more room over there."

Mom nods, then looks at me. "Where would you prefer to have the party, Wren? At my house, or here, with Dad?"

I do a tiny gasp. She called him *Dad* this time, not *your dad*. It probably seems like a little thing, but it's a big deal to me.

"Could we have the sleepover at our house?" I ask Mom. "And then ride bikes here the next day?"

"Fine by me," Mom says.

Dad nods. "I could borrow a boat and some poles. Take you girls fishing on the lake."

I butt-hop with happiness.

"That's settled, then," Mom says. "I'll put it on the schedule."

Dad takes another slice of pizza. "I'll start digging worms."

Later, after Mom tucks me in and goes back home, I reach for my phone. There's a text from Amber!

Call me 2MORO!

I smile and send one back.

Oh. Kay!

Then I click up the dictionary on my phone and type in the word *family*.

Family
• Descendants of a common ancestor
• Persons united by similar convictions
• A basic social unit, consisting of parents and their children, whether dwelling together or not

I read the last part out loud to Shakespeare. "*Whether dwelling together or not.*"

"Mew," he says, curling up next to me on my bunk.

Dear Diary,

Lots of things have changed since my first week of school. Big things, like living in two places, and getting a new favorite teacher, and making new friends, and finally being brave enough to tell Amber the truth. And little things, like starting a unicorn collection, and getting a bunk bed, and keeping a diary. Probably more things will change too. And I keep thinking of new questions. Like, what snacks should I buy for my sleepover? How many fish will we catch? Will Dad really let me paint my room orange? Will he come to Thanksgiving at G-ma's house? Will Mom ever sit under the table with me again? Could we all go to Mount Rushmore next summer? Could Amber come along?

Ms. Little says there's no such thing as a silly question.

I'm glad because I still have lots of questions to ask.

The End